Get down to the bookstore
for more Bad Dog books!

Bad Dog and That Hollywood Hoohah
Bad Dog and Those Crazy Martians
Bad Dog and the Curse of the President's Knee

GOES BARKTASTIC!

MARTIN CHATTERTON

SCHOLASTIC INC.

New York   Toronto   London   Auckland   Sydney
Mexico City   New Delhi   Hong Kong   Buenos Aires

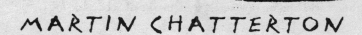

ISBN 0-439-67714-9

All rights reserved. Published by Scholastic Inc., 557 Broadway, New York, NY 10012, by arrangement with Scholastic Ltd.

12 11 10 9 8 7 6 5 4 3 2 1   5 6 7 8 9 10 / 0

Printed in the U.S.A.   40
First Scholastic U.S.A. printing, August 2005

CHAPTER 1

DIE ANOTHER DAY

The name's Dog. Long pause and raise one eyebrow. Bad Dog.

OK. Where do we start with this one? Well, perhaps I could begin by saying that you are looking at the dog who single-handedly (with the aid of my trusted sidekick, the Reverend Bentley Sweetlord the Fourth) saved the world. Or, to be precise, saved the doggy world. But of course, all that saving the world stuff is all in a day's work when you are a mega-cool super-spy and International Pooch of Mystery . . .

It all began a couple of months back, right here on Z-Block at the City Dog Pound. If I'd been running a competition for The Very Worst Day of My Life, there's no question that day would have won hands down. And believe me, I've had plenty of *really* bad days so that'd be some stiff competition. It'd help if you knew who I am and where I was, I guess, although if you haven't heard of me by now, where've you been? After all, I'm the dog who shot to fame in Hollywood, set paw on Mars, saved the life of the

President (of the United States, not the President of the Milwaukee Chapter of Honorable Elks, just in case you were wondering), and went to number one as the first doggy rapper of all time. You *musta* heard of me.

This place, the place where I have spent more time than I care to think about, is Z-Block. You know all the dogs that no one wants? All the mutts, the strays, the street dogs? They end up here where they get — how can I put this? Where they get killed. Yep, that's right. If no one comes to pick us doggies up, we get to go through that green door at the end of the cell block. We aren't certain what goes on behind the green door, but we are certain about one thing: Once you've been through that door, there's no coming back. You hear what I'm saying?

And on this particular day — y'know, The Very Worst Day of My Life — it was my turn.

I'd been close before, very close. In fact I've been so close, so many times, that for a time I thought I was too lucky to ever make that final trip with Fester, the zit-ridden, nacho-munching, dipstick humanoid in charge of us pooches down on Z-Block.

I was wrong.

"Hey, hombre. You lookin' down in the mouth, YOU FLEA-BITTEN SON OF A SKUNK!"

I looked down at the dog who had spoken, a wizened runt of a chihuahua called Big T who was sitting in the cell next to me scratching his butt. He was so small that when he'd first come onto the block, I thought the Pound had admitted a chunky rat by mistake. I hadn't paid him much attention, mainly because he spouted so much nonsense.

"Beware the men in white, my frien'! Keep your mouth closed! Don't bark! They will suck it out, I think, yes! Cold, so cold in space! I HATE YOU, STINKY CHEESEBREATH MUTT-PIG!"

See what I mean?

Big T had been spouting his stuff ever since he'd arrived. He wasn't alone. Most of the new arrivals talked like this whenever they weren't fighting, drooling, or pooping.

Over the last couple of months the green door had been opened more times than a daily newspaper due to the unusually high number of pooches coming onto Z-Block. The new dogs were different somehow from the rest of us. They were nasty, snarling street-hounds who would take a bite out of you as soon as look at you.

Rumors were flying around the yard of strange doggy behavior going on in the outside world. Dogs attacking their "owners," dogs stealing food from babies, pooping everywhere, even *refusing to fetch sticks*, if you can imagine such a thing. Police dogs weren't sniffing anything out, guide dogs for the blind were steering their unsuspecting masters onto

highways and airport runways. St. Bernard rescue dogs were leaving skiers stuck in avalanches. Even the Queen of England had been cornered by a pack of her own corgis and given a nasty nip on the royal rear before being rescued by her grandson in a helicopter.

The result of all this doggy delinquency? Overflowing dog pounds as a tidal wave of unwanted pooches washed up everywhere. Oh, and one more thing: A lot of these bad dogs were bald as eggs. Figure that one out.

To be honest, although part of me had thought about the strange happenings in the canine world, most of my attention had been taken up by my soon-to-happen trip to oblivion. I ignored Big T's ramblings and concentrated on thinking about sinking my fangs into Fester.

"C'mon, homies," sneered Fester, referring to my most recent escapade in the wonderful world of hip-hop. "Today's the day."

He pointed at the green door with the end of his mop.

I looked at my very good pal, the Reverend Bentley Sweetlord the Fourth, and was about to say something when Fester pointed the broom his way.

"You, too, Lassie," he snickered. "We got a two-for-one deal going today. You both get to go through the door."

We looked at  each other. This was it. We were going to go together. It was something, at least, and I used all my inner strength to help me go with as much dignity and cool as possible.

"NNNNNNOOOOOOOOOOOOOOOOOO!!!!!"
I wailed. "There's been a terrible mistake!"

Fester bent down to pry loose my paws, which were wrapped tightly around the doorknob of my cell. I clung on like a barnacle and howled like a . . . well, like a dog.

Fester grabbed Bentley's collar.

"Get yer filthy paws offa me, copper!" snarled Bentley. "I'll go under my own steam, y'dig?"

Fester let Bentley walk forward. I straightened up and took a deep breath.

The door stood in front of us, green, rusted, and terrifying. I shook paws with Bentley, and Fester drew back the iron bolts.

"Goodbye, old friend!" I croaked. We stepped

through into total darkness and then we were falling, falling, falling . . .

There was a soft rush of cold air, as if someone had opened a door somewhere, and the lights went on, temporarily blinding us. When my sight returned I saw that we were on the floor of a large, completely white room lit by harsh strip lights. Fester sat behind a white desk in the center of the room. Instead of his normal scuzz-spattered overalls he was wearing a perfectly tailored black suit. His normally lank hair was combed back into a neat ponytail. In the chair next to him sat a very old dog with a patch over one eye and a sour look on his face.

"Are we dead?" I managed to bark. My throat felt like it had been on a fire-breathing course.

"If we are," said Bentley, nodding towards Fester, "it sure ain't heaven if this cat's still hangin' round."

I was about to say something when Fester barked.

"No, gentlemen," he said in flawless doggyspeak, "you aren't dead. Not yet. However, you have been unconscious for several hours. That's just a tiresome side effect, but at least it gave me time to change out of those repulsive clothes."

We stared open-mouthed at Fester's newfound ability to talk Dog, but before we could quiz him about this interesting talent he stood and walked around the desk. He raised a hand to the top of his greasy hair and tugged sharply at something on his scalp. With a sound like a melon being sat on by a howler monkey juggling a plank of wood (trust me, you had to be there), Fester peeled his head neatly down the middle to reveal the head of a crossbred lurcher.

The dog inside Fester continued to peel back

his . . . his what? . . . his skin until it dropped to the floor and the dog stepped out, leaving Fester lying on the floor in a rubbery heap.

"Of course getting out of Fester's skin is even better," said the dog.

My eyes rolled up into my head and everything went kinda swimmy as I blacked out for the second time that day.

"Wha . . . wher . . . ng?" I asked smoothly as my vision came back.

"You all right?" asked the dog who'd been inside Fester. Instantly I remembered why I'd fainted in the first place and every-thing started to drift again.

"Oh no," said the dog, slapping me a quick one around the chops. "Not this time, soldier. We've got too much to do."

He and Bentley lifted me up off the cold white floor and sat me down in one of two black leather chairs facing the desk. Bentley settled his bulky form into the other and gave me a Look. Needless to say, Bentley hadn't batted an eye during the whole Fester skin-peeling thing and looked as cool as an Eskimo fashion model in a swimsuit standing on a block of ice in Alaska.

"Let me introduce myself," said Fester/the dog from behind the desk. "Around here I'm known as Agent 4. This gentleman here is Mr. Smith." Agent 4 gestured towards the small, one-eyed dog, who nodded slightly towards us. "Welcome to the CIA."

"CIA?" said Bentley, narrowing his eyes.

"Canine Intelligence Agency," said Mr. Smith in a gravelly voice. "We're here to look after doggy . . . interests."

"And where exactly is this 'CIA'?" said Bentley.

Smith looked up.

"We're three floors below the basement level of Z-Block," he said.

I looked at him in disbelief.

"You mean all that time we were sitting up there, this placed was down here?"

He nodded.

Bentley's face was thunder.

"All that time we were stuck in the slammer you guys knew about it and did . . . nothing?"

Mr. Smith nodded again. He was in danger of looking like one of those nodding dogs you see in the backs of cars. "Precisely, Mr. Sweetlord."

"It's *Reverend* Sweetlord," said Bentley in a dangerous tone.

Mr. Smith simply smiled and said nothing. At least he didn't nod. "And what about Fester?" I asked. "Is he, you know . . . dead?" I wasn't worried about him, you understand, but after a couple of years on the block I felt the need to know the exact status of ole zit-face. Mr. Smith shook his head. "No. Mr. Mifflin, or 'Fester' as you know him, is being, erm, *held* at our HDC in Utah."

"HDC?"

"Human Detention Center," Smith explained. "It's where we take humans we have identified as unsympathetic to the canine cause. We, um, re-educate them."

"You mean there's a place where dogs lock up humans?" I couldn't think of anything that would give me more satisfaction than seeing Fester held under lock and key by a bunch of dogs.

Mr. Smith waved his paw. "It's of no importance."

"What about the thing you did . . . that whole head-unzipping trip?" said Bentley, looking at Agent 4.

"I merely utilized advanced prosthetic conceal-ment techniques. It's common practice."

I looked blank. "He wore a disguise," said Bentley, seeing my puzzlement. "I knew that," I said, although I could see that I might need a translator if Agent 4 kept on talking like that.

Mr. Smith paused for a moment and then leaned forward.

"Anything you see or hear from me and this organization must remain FYPO, understand?"

"FYPO?" I said.

"For Your Paws Only," said Smith. "We are a top-secret organization dedicated to protecting canine . . . *interests* on the local, national, and international global stage."

I looked blank again.

"They look after doggy stuff," said Bentley.

"I knew that," I said huffily.

Smith stood up.

"I'll explain on the way," he said, gesturing for us to follow.

"Explain what?" I said as the four of us walked towards a set of elevator doors.

"Your mission," said Mr. Smith, pressing his paw against the heat-sensitive, paw-shaped pad bolted to the wall. "To save the world."

CHAPTER 2

MISSION IMPOSSIBLE

The elevator doors slid shut with a soft thunk, Agent 4 pressed a button, and we began to drop at what seemed like an incredible speed. Agent 4 pressed another button and the elevator slowed and then halted. The doors hissed softly open to reveal an enormous, hangarlike room filled with activity. Dogs in white coats and wearing protective glasses trotted past, examining clipboards. Mysterious bits of equipment were being tested; banks of computers filled the air with a busy electronic hum. Across one wall was a huge display showing a map of the world dotted here and there with blinking red and green lights. A line of keen-eyed dachshunds watched a bank of TV monitors and made notes. I noticed a bunch of Jack Russells dressed in ninja uniforms rappelling down one wall.

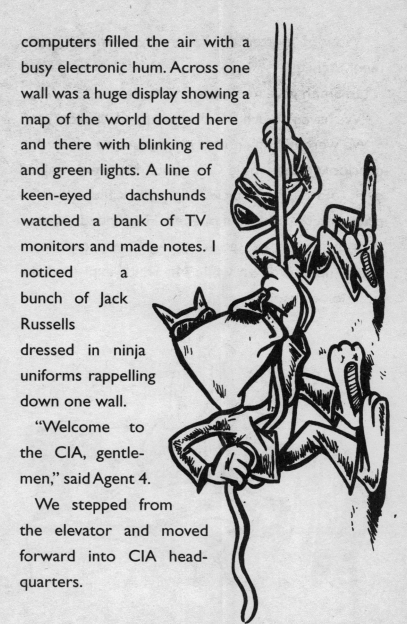

"Welcome to the CIA, gentlemen," said Agent 4.

We stepped from the elevator and moved forward into CIA headquarters.

"Wow," I muttered. "You really fixed this basement up nice."

Mr. Smith gave me a sour look.

"We haven't much time," he snapped. "Follow me."

We were led up an iron gangway to an office that overlooked the whole CIA layout. Mr. Smith walked over to a desk and picked up a thick file, which he placed on the table and opened. He nodded towards two chairs and we sat down. Agent 4 paced impatiently up and down while Mr. Smith explained the situation to us.

"You'll have noticed a certain amount of unusual activity in the Pound, no doubt? A substantial escalation in the quantity of antisocial canines incarcerated exhibiting profound antisocial tendencies and incipient alopecia?"

I pretended I knew what he was talking about.

"A lot of bad, bald dogs have been put in the slammer," Bentley explained, as if he was talking to a dim pup of two.

"I knew that," I said.

Mr. Smith pointed to the file.

"This is information we have been collecting ever since the numbers began to rise. We have deep-cover agents placed in every dog pound in North America. A few months ago these agents began to send in reports of canines acting . . . strangely. I thought it was worth looking into, even if some dogs around here didn't think so." He shot a narrow look at Agent 4 and I detected a certain frostiness between Mr. Smith and the dog formerly known as Fester.

"We heard about the strange dogs," said Bentley, nodding. "Lot of weirdness going down out there, brother."

"All these behavior changes were disturbing enough, without the stories the dogs were telling about being abducted by aliens and experimented upon," Mr. Smith continued. "We knew this was non-sense, of course. None of our canine space patrols reported anything unusual as far out as Uranus."

I sniggered. *Uranus.* That one always cracks me up.

Mr. Smith looked at me sadly and shook his head.

"You have space patrols?" asked Bentley. "Like, dogs in space?"

My ears pricked up. I knew all about dogs in space from my time as a space dog on Mars (it's a long story . . . go buy the book).

Mr. Smith nodded impatiently.

"Of course. It's not important." He looked up at us with his one good eye. "But what may be important is this."

He slipped a sheet from the file and pushed it across the desk towards us.

It was an aerial photo-
graph of a large
building sur-
rounded by a
number of
smaller ones, all
set in a snowy
wasteland.

"So?" said Bentley. "What's so special about this place?"

"We aren't sure yet," said Mr. Smith. "Which is where you two come in."

"Us?" I said, but Mr. Smith was talking again.

"We picked up an unusual amount of XBA on our satellites and pinpointed it to this compound."

He flicked a paw at the photograph.

"XBA?" I said. This guy sure liked flinging those initials everywhere.

"Extreme Barking Activity," said Mr. Smith. "This compound is in Northern Siberia, far inside the Arctic Circle. It's so remote that even the Russians don't know it's there. We need two agents to parachute in at night, get past the heavy security, find out what's happening, and then escape across the icy Siberian tundra."

"It sounds like a suicide mission," said Bentley.

"Which is why we can't waste two perfectly good agents," said Agent 4, chiming in from over in the corner. "We need to get two new recruits, give them a little basic spy training and a few gadgets, drop them over Siberia, and hope for the best. It's probably all a wild goose chase."

Mr. Smith looked at Agent 4 frostily.

"So where are you going to find two dogs dumb enough to go along with such a crazy idea?" I snickered.

Agent 4 looked at me, raised an eyebrow, and smiled. The Reverend looked at me with a sour expression on his face.

"Take a wild guess," said Agent 4, laughing in a weird way. "Har har har."

The penny dropped. We were going to Siberia.

CHAPTER 3

SPIES LIKE US

Mr. Smith and Agent 4 outlined the situation on our way to the CIA equipment store. We could either accept the mission and fly to the mysterious dog-torture place in Northern Siberia or head back to Z-Block and take our chances with the humans. When he put it like that . . .

We crossed the floor of the CIA HQ PDQ ("pretty darn quick" — like I said, these guys loved their initials) and headed down in the elevator once more into what looked like a laboratory. Various dogs moved purposefully about the place carrying clipboards and wearing horn-rimmed glasses.

"Mr. Don't," said Mr. Smith to a large, clumsy-looking dog bent over a microscope.

"Good morning, sir!" said Don't, making a final tap on the laptop keyboard next to the microscope. "I see you have our two dummi — our two volunteers."

He straightened up and I gasped in astonishment. Mr. Don't bore a striking resemblance to a cartoon dog famous for his cowardice and love of snacks.

"Hey!" I said pointing. "You look just like that dog on the cartoon! Y'know, the one that gets trapped in the old spooky fairground with that hippy human guy —"

"I know the type," said Don't, waving his hand dismissively. "A waste of a beautiful mind."

"Mr. Don't will look after you," said Mr. Smith. "I'll be back to see you off later this evening. The flight leaves at 20:00 hours sharp. Come with me, Agent 4."

He turned on his heel and walked away, with Agent 4 marching briskly behind. I watched them leave and turned to see Don't brandishing a huge hypodermic needle and looking at me.

"This will hurt quite a bit," he said.

"Whoa!" I squeaked, backing away. "Not so fast, Mr. Don't! Besides, aren't you supposed to say 'this won't hurt at all'?"

"It's a tracking device," said Don't. "And I merely pointed out the scientific facts concerning the pain levels."

Bentley stepped forward and thrust out a massive arm.

"Spike me," he growled at Don't.

Don't inserted the tracking device into the Reverend, who didn't bat an eyelid. I was so brave when it was my turn that it only took three of Don't's assistants to hold me down.

"This tracking chip enables us to pinpoint exactly where you are at any given time. It will also relay data about your heartbeat, temperature, and other essential information," said Don't. "It could save your life."

He picked up a couple of dog collars.

"Hey, doc," said Bentley. "The tracker is one thing but I ain't wearin' no collar, understand?"

I wasn't too crazy about the idea, either, to be honest. No self-respecting yard dog is ever entirely comfortable with a collar. It means you belong to someone.

"This is no ordinary collar, gentlemen," said Mr. Don't. "Observe."

He slipped it around his own neck and pressed

one of the collar studs. With a soft hum, he rose several feet into the air.

"Antigravity device," said Don't, dropping back down to the floor.

He pressed another stud and a slim microphone curled around and positioned itself in front of his mouth.

"Radio transmitter for instant communication with HQ."

"Man," I said to the Reverend, "this is pretty cool!"

Don't pushed another of the studs, and this time two small rocket launchers sprang from either side of the collar. Don't swiveled to face a target positioned against a brick wall and pressed a button on the collar. Two missiles streaked out of the launchers and exploded dead center of the target in a ball of flame and smoke.

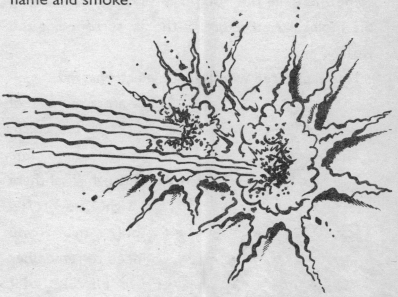

"A trifle showy, I feel," said Don't. "But quite effective."

He pressed the stud again and the rocket launchers slid back into their concealed slots.

"This is one I am really proud of," said Don't. "It's brand new and it can be a bit patchy performance-wise but it's still pretty good."

He pressed a switch and immediately disappeared into thin air.

"Invisibility device," said Don't's voice, floating somewhere in the room. "Works by rearranging the molecular structure of the air surrounding the wearer."

He reappeared with a gentle electronic fizz.

"There are a number of other devices in the collar, but we don't have time to go through all of them right now. The only thing you need to remember is NEVER, EVER press the red button on the back of the collar."

"Why?" I said.

"Do you know, I can't remember," said Mr. Don't. "But I know it's very, very bad. Very bad indeed. You'll have to check the manual."

He passed two of the collars over together with a slim, dog-eared (excuse me) collection of scrappily assembled photocopied pages.

"*This* is the manual?" said Bentley, holding it by a corner.

Don't nodded.

"We didn't have much time," he said.

We fitted our collars a little nervously. Bentley's was a little too tight, as his neck was roughly the size of a redwood tree.

"AAAAARGH!" yelled Bentley as he fiddled with the collar. "I accidentally pressed the red button! Run for your lives!"

Mr. Don't and I screamed and leaped straight into

a metal wastebasket before we realized that Bentley was joking.

"Ha ha," I said. "Very funny."

Don't climbed out of the wastebasket and sifted through a large box. From inside he produced a pair of thick-framed black glasses and handed them to me.

"My eyes are fine," I said.

"Just try them," said Don't.

I slipped them on. There were some tiny switches at the side, which turned the glasses into powerful binoculars, X-ray vision, or heat-detection sensors, not to mention a 400-gigabyte onboard computer with a liquid plasma display screen and interactive all-terrain software. (No, I don't know what that means, either, but it looked really cool.) Bentley had a similar pair, only with dark lenses. Typical, he gets the street-cool shades and I get to look like Nerd of the Month.

I decided to test the antigravity device and pressed a button on the collar. I rose up at something like the speed of sound and only avoided planting my head through the ceiling by turning off the device at the last moment. I fell straight back down again and landed on Bentley, who crashed back into a huge pile of expensive-looking equipment. We sat up, brushing bits of circuit board and glass off us.

Don't folded his arms and sighed.

"I guess you'll have to do," he said.

Chapter 4

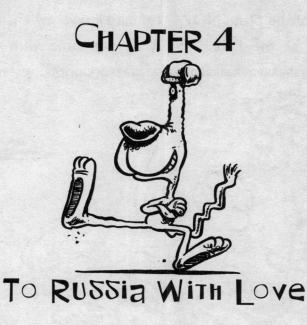

To Russia With Love

It wasn't that I was scared, you understand. I just didn't feel like jumping out of the plane at that particular moment. I was wedged in the doorway of the blacked-out, radar-proof CIA transport plane, paws braced against the frame and eyes tightly closed. I could feel the rush of freezing air pulling me out of the plane 7,000 yards above Northern Siberia.

"No, thanks," I said in response to Bentley's suggestion that I get my skinny, yellow-bellied carcass out of the plane NOW. "I think I'll take my chances back at the Pound, if it's all the same with you chaaaaaaaaaaaaaaaaaaaaaaaaaaaaaaaaaapppppppppppssssssss sssssss!!!"

You'll have noticed that last part came out in a long scream. This was because as I was about to finish speaking, Bentley planted a massive paw on my back and kicked me out into icy black nothingness. I continued screaming for, oh, perhaps an hour or two, when I became conscious of something in the back of my mind. I was sure there was something I was supposed to do when it got to this part, something really important, but for the life of me I couldn't quite think what that Really Important Thing might be.

"Your parachute!" screamed Bentley as he hurtled out of the blackness past my left shoulder. "OPEN YOUR PARACHUTE, YOU NUMB-SKULL!"

Of course. That was it. The Really Important Thing was that I should remember to open my parachute, otherwise I would smash into the ground at a speed of 200 mph and disintegrate into a soggy mess, which is a bad thing, right? I frantically tried to remember how exactly I was supposed to open my 'chute. Back at HQ, Agent 4 had demonstrated this to me several times but, to be honest, I hadn't been listening because I had been investigating a marvelously interesting stench coming from my butt area. This was something I was beginning to regret as the concrete-hard Siberian ice fields were now getting closer at a quite ridiculous rate. I decided to do what generations of my family had done in these situations: panic.

I pulled anything and everything on my multi-pocketed (and incredibly fab) new white flightsuit.

I ripped open pockets and tugged on bits of kit attached here and there. Nothing. I passed Bentley as he pulled open his 'chute. He yelled something at me as I shot past, but I couldn't make it out. Then, just as death seemed to be my only other option, I yanked on a metal hoop and was jerked upwards as my lovely, lovely parachute snapped open.

It was none too soon, either. I was so close to the ground that I could make out individual trees and, although I was no longer traveling incredibly fast, as the ground drew closer I could see that I was still in for a bumpy landing. I remembered the manual and dragged it out of one of my pockets.

"Parachute landings, parachute landings," I muttered, flicking through the pages. "Ah, here we are, page eight: 'The Correct Procedure for a Successful Solution to an Airborne Vertical Trajectory Descent Utilizing Manual Flight Equipment.'"

Mr. Don't had certainly had time to write long headings for this manual, I thought, just as I hit the ground. I flipped over and luckily managed to use my mouth as an anchor by filling it with snow as the parachute dragged me across the tundra.

I slowed down after bumping over some very hard pieces of ice, which seemed magically drawn towards the squashier parts of my body. Still, at least I was back on land once again. I lay on my back, breathing the icy air deeply, and began to relax as I watched the stars.

The stars were instantly blotted out by a large, dark shape as the Reverend Bentley cushioned his landing by planting a pair of monstrous paws on my belly. All the air left my body as Bentley bounced off me and landed softly in a snowdrift.

"Nothing to it," he said, brushing flakes of snow off his suit. "Piece of cake."

"Neeeeeeh," I said. "Fffffffeeeeeh. Heeeeeergh."

"Sorry, brother," said Bentley. "You ain't makin' any sense, man. Get your act together."

If I'd had any strength I'd have whacked the Reverend there and then, I swear.

He unzipped his parachute as I rolled around on the snow like a landed fish. Eventually my breathing returned to normal, leaving just the forty-seven broken ribs to deal with.

"You all done?" said Bentley. "Can we get moving now? Seeing as how we *are* in *the* coldest place on earth?"

Now that he mentioned it, and now that the pain had gone down a notch, I did notice that the weather was a tad on the cool side. A strong wind cut through our hi-tech winter protection gear and icy darts of snow smacked into our faces. From a distance came a blood-curdling howl. It seemed to be coming from an inky-black forested area off to our left.

"Just wolves," said Bentley.

"Whaddya mean, *just* wolves?" I said through chattering teeth.

"Wolves are just big dogs, sorta," said Bentley. "It ain't nothing."

"Yeah, those Siberian timberwolves'll probably just invite us to pull up an easy chair, sit back, and watch the ball game, right?"

Bentley wasn't listening. He flipped a switch on his shades and pointed across to the forest.

"That way."

"Are you sure?" I said, eyeing the black trees where the howl had come from. "My instinct says this way." I pointed in the opposite direction.

"Ain't nothing that way till you hit Vladivostok," said Bentley.

"So?" I said. "What's wrong with Vladivostok? Sounds fine to me right now. Besides, since when did you become such an almighty expert on the location of secret compounds?"

I was speaking to myself. Bentley had set off across the snow towards the trees. I looked around wistfully in the direction of Vladivostok, then legged it across the snow towards Bentley and the Siberian timberwolves.

"Could you give me a little space, dude?" said Bentley when we'd traveled a few minutes into the forest. I reluctantly let go of his leg, to which I'd been clamped.

"No problem," I said. "I was, er, just checking you hadn't damaged your knee when I hit it with my stomach —"

"Shhh!" said Bentley.

He tilted his head to one side and listened. I did the same. There it was. Some distance away but unmistakable: the sound of barking!

"We must be getting close to that compound," said Bentley. "Let's get moving. The sooner we get to the bottom of this, the sooner we'll be back in civilization."

I didn't exactly think of Z-Block as civilization, but this deep into a spooky Siberian forest I wasn't going to split hairs with the Rev. We upped the pace towards the dogs.

CHAPTER 5

THE POOCH WHO CAME IN FROM THE COLD

There it was. The building we'd seen earlier that day on Agent 4's desk back at CIA HQ.

The compound lay bathed in white light. Secret though it might be, whoever was in control wasn't too worried about nosy neighbors. Since we were 600 snowbound miles from any sort of a town, I guess they thought that was unlikely.

We lay on a bank of snow at the edge of the forest, looking down on the compound through our zoom-lens specs. It lay in a huge clearing, deep inside the forest. To one side of the buildings was a runway on which sat three fat transport planes, sort of like whales, only with wings. There was a lot of frantic activity going on around them. Heavily laden forklift trucks moved out to the planes and returned empty. They were obviously sending something out from the compound. Up close we could hear frantic barking coming from somewhere deep inside the complex. It wasn't a happy sound.

"This is great!" I said to Bentley. "Real spy stuff! I feel like I'm in the movies!"

Bentley grunted. He was a nice pooch at heart but I sometimes wished he would lighten up a little — you know, kick back and enjoy the moment. I guess his street survival skills were coming into play.

"We gotta take this real easy, brother," he said. "There's something screwy going on, I can feel it. This place don't feel right here. We gotta be careful."

I nodded, fiddling with my new collar, which had begun to itch.

"Uh-huh," I muttered. "Careful."

"We can't let them know we are here," said Bentley. "Surprise is our best weapon."

"Mmm, yep," I said, tugging at my collar. "Surprise. Yep."

I scratched furiously at my collar. Man, this was one *itchy* choker. Suddenly the two rocket launchers popped out and swiveled into position.

Bentley looked at me and raised his eyebrows.

"Don't worry," I said. "I just pressed the wrong button. I'll put them ba —"

Before I could finish what I was saying, there was a deafening explosion and two heat-seeking smart missiles streaked towards the compound. They veered off towards the nearest source of heat, which happened to be one of the forklift trucks rolling towards a plane. There was a shout and the driver of the forklift whirled around seconds before impact. He yelped and scrambled clear of his vehicle just as the missiles hit home with a dull *whump*. The forklift exploded into a thousand pieces and rained down in a fiery mass onto the runway. The boxes it had been carrying scattered their contents far and wide, so far in fact that some of them landed close to our position. There was a brief moment of total silence.

"Ooops," I said.

Bentley looked at me.

"Nice and quiet, I said," muttered Bentley. "Careful, I said."

I picked up one of the objects that had landed next to us and looked at it. It was still smoking and part of the labeling had burned off, but I could still see what it was: a can of dog food. I had just started to think about why there would be a top-secret dog-food plant deep in the Siberian forest when Bentley  hooked a paw around my neck and dragged me to my feet.

"We'd better skedaddle," he said, nodding at the compound. Alarms were sounding and guards poured out the doors, pointing at where the missiles had come from. (I figured they had probably noticed us.)

We rolled down the bank, back into the cover of the forest, and set off in the direction of Vladivostok as fast as our doggy legs would carry us across the snow. Behind us we could hear a roar of engines. I risked a look back. The guards were climbing onto sleek white snowmobiles and zipping up the hill towards us, gunning the engines as they tore through the snow and ice. Snowmobiles! We couldn't outrun them, and we could soon hear them getting closer on all sides. We caught glimpses of them through the trees. We ran in circles as they got nearer. It looked like we were going to get caught.

Bentley prepared to put up a fight.

"I ain't going without taking some of them with me," he snarled.

Suddenly I had a brainstorm. I don't get many, but when I do they tend to be doozies. I started to fiddle with my collar again.

"What're you doin', man?" said Bentley. "You're gonna blow your fool head clean off this time."

I wasn't listening. I flipped through the manual and found what I was looking for, then reached up and pressed a button. Instantly I disappeared.

Bentley did a doubletake and then smiled.

"You know, brother," he said, "sometimes you surprise me."

He pressed the same button on his collar and disappeared, too, just a few seconds before the first guards from the compound burst through the trees. We watched as they raced past us on roaring snowmobiles just a few short yards away. As they zoomed off on a wild goose chase, I turned to see a set of Bentley-shaped pawprints moving back towards the compound.

"Hey!" I hissed. "Where are you going?"

"Back to the compound," said Bentley. "We've got some unfinished business."

I shrugged and crunched across the snow in Bentley's direction. Invisible apart from the footprints we left behind, we moved down the snowbank towards the brightly lit compound.

Inside it was still complete pandemonium. Smoke billowed up from the wreckage of the forklift and guards ran purposefully here and there. The sirens were still sounding and extra guards had been posted on the barred entrance. Invisible as we were, I still felt like I was walking a tightrope across Niagara Falls.

"Any ideas?" whispered a voice in my ear. I jumped a couple of hundred feet in the air.

"Bentley!" I snarled. "You almost gave me a heart attack, man! Quit sneakin' up on people like that!"

"Yeah, yeah," said Bentley. "So, do you have any ideas?"

I cocked my ears and listened. The dogs inside were still barking.

"Let's see if we can spring those guys," I said. "They sound like they need to be rescued by a couple of highly trained, armed-to-the-teeth Special Forces CIA operatives."

"Yeah," said Bentley. "But until they turn up, I guess we'll just have to do. Heh, heh, heh."

"Very funny," I said, pointing over at a door set into one of the buildings nearby. "There."

"Where?" said Bentley.

I was about to get mad when I realized we were still invisible.

"Over there. The door."

Bentley didn't reply but I saw his pawprints heading towards the door. I trotted after him. To my

surprise, the door wasn't locked, and we slipped
inside the building.

It was a lot warmer inside, probably just above
freezing, but since it was cold enough outside to
freeze a volcano, it felt positively tropical. Suddenly
Bentley reappeared right in front of me.

"What are you doing?" I hissed. "Turn it back on!"

Then I realized that I was now visible, too. I
pressed the button again but nothing happened.

"Piece o' junk," said Bentley.

I checked the manual again.

"Only works for short periods of time, it says
here," I said. "You have to wait an hour for the
whatchamacallit to work again."

"Let's get moving then, brother," said Bentley.
"We're kind of noticeable."

We headed through a large warehouse that was stacked to the ceiling with the crates we'd seen heading onto the transport planes. They were all filled with cans of the same dog food that had landed on the snowbank next to me. There must have been ten million cans in this warehouse alone, and I'd counted four buildings exactly like this one.

"That's a whole lot of doggy chow," Bentley whistled softly. "But why all the secrecy, all the guards and wires and alarms and stuff?"

"Perhaps Britney Spears lives here?" I suggested.

Bentley gave me a Look.

"Only kiddin'," I said.

We reached the end of one of the warehouse aisles without seeing anyone. I figured they were all out in the snow, chasing after shadows.

A thicker, more solid-looking door stood in front of us, and from behind it the sound of the dogs was even louder. I tried the handle but it didn't give at all. Bentley gave it a kick and it flew open.

An iron gangway ran from the door around a large laboratory-looking room. In the center were various computers and pieces of scientific-looking equipment. Lined along the walls were cages full of dogs. Bald dogs. As soon as they saw us, the laboratory fell silent.

"Er, hi fellas," I said, holding my hand up and speaking into the silence. "Panic over. We're here to rescue you."

I didn't get the reaction I expected. Instead of the chorus of "oh-thank-you-kind-CIA-agent," all the dogs burst out laughing. They slapped the floor with their paws and tears rolled down their faces as they all had a good long belly laugh. That was strange enough, but the laughter worried me. It had a strange quality to it: nasty, vicious.

"Now wait just a minute," said Bentley, but they weren't listening.

"BITE ME!" yelled one.

"YOUR MOTHER HAS FLEAS!" yapped another.

Several of the dogs started throwing water bowls at us and banging on their cages.

"What's going on?" I asked Bentley, who was ignoring the racket and examining some of the laboratory equipment.

"Look," he said, pointing to a bench.

At one end were a number of the cans of dog food we'd seen stacked in the warehouse. They had been opened and had little white labels stuck on them. Small bits of dog food were being checked in complicated-looking machines.

"It's the food, brother," said Bentley. "These dudes are getting tested. Whoever's in charge of this place is testing some kind of wacko food on the dogs. I think that's why they're all acting like this."

"What about the hair?" I asked. "And why would anyone want to make dog food that does this?" I gestured around the room.

"Maybe the hair's just a side effect?" said Bentley. "Whatever they're putting in there causes the bad behavior and makes the hair fall out, something like that. Perhaps the bad behavior is what these guys are looking for? As for why — well, I ain't got a clue."

The sound of the dogs was deafening, so I could hardly hear myself think. Then, quite suddenly, the room fell silent.

"What a relie —" I started to speak, then Bentley nudged me in the ribs and pointed up towards a large window above the iron gangway that looked out across the whole laboratory. Standing there was a huge man holding a small cat. When I say "huge," what I mean is that this dude was calorifically challenged. His white suit could have been altered to provide the sails for an ocean-going yacht and still have enough left to make a sizeable tent. He had narrow green eyes and greased-back hair tied in a ponytail. A small, neatly trimmed goatee surrounded a cruel mouth with wet lips.

The cat he held was even more disgusting — a thin, vicious streak of furry feline fury who glowered at us with undisguised hate. I growled back at the cat, the fur on my back rising. Have I mentioned how much I hate cats? It's the one thing that makes me lose it, and I was starting to lose it right now.

"Easy, tiger," Bentley said softly.

He nodded towards the group. Behind the fat man and his cat stood a giant of a man dressed entirely in black and wearing a bowler hat. He grinned as the fat man said something to him and revealed a set of steel teeth. Iron Gob left the room and started out down the gangway towards us.

"See what you mean," I said to Bentley. "Time to go."

Bentley nodded, fiddled with his shades (make a note of this, it's important later on), and we headed for the door. Before we could get there it flew open and four heavily armed guards burst through. We backed up the steps, only to find the way cut off by Iron Gob, grinning like a maniac.

We were trapped.

I quickly formed a cunning plan, which involved selling them my grandmother, when I felt myself rising into the air. I opened my eyes (I had screwed them tightly shut when I thought I was about to get marmalized) to find Bentley shooting straight up towards the roof, holding me by the scruff of my neck. I was amazed at his new-found ability to fly until he reached down and flicked the button on my collar and I remembered all the gizmos Don't had built in. Suddenly I, too, was completely weightless.

"My turn for the bright ideas," said Bentley.

"Not a bad one, either, Your Holiness," I said as we drifted away from the bad guys. "I could get used to wearing this collar."

Bentley smiled but we didn't get time to talk about the merits of collar-wearing because everyone below started blazing away with machine guns. The air filled with the roar of a thousand rounds of hot lead all heading our way. I closed my eyes and waited for one of the bullets to rearrange my life permanently, but before that could happen we smashed through the skylight at the top of the lab and shot out into the freezing black sky like a couple of hairy rockets.

Bentley flipped a reading light on at the side of his shades and consulted the manual as we zipped away from the compound.

"What are you doing?" I said. "Let's just fly all the way back to HQ!"

Bentley shook his head and pointed at the manual.

"We can't, brother. Says here that we only got a couple of minutes before it runs outta power. We have to set down."

We drifted down, controlling our speed by twiddling the collar studs, and landed in the forest.

"Oh great," I said looking around at the darkness. "The spooky forest. My favorite."

"What do you think?" asked the Reverend.

"I was hoping you'd have some divine inspiration, dude, because I'm comin' up with absolutely zip."

We looked around blankly at the wall of black trees. As I was temporarily unable to come up with a fab idea, I decided to fill in the time by taking a leak against one of the nearby trees. I was just about to get busy when the ground seemed to tremble and there was a long, very deep growl from somewhere in the woods.

Somewhere close.

I peered fearfully into the blackness and saw a pair of glowing eyes watching me. With hardly any panic at all I flipped a button on my new specs to switch on the night vision. Immediately the world turned a milky green-white, and I could see a huge furry shape looking at me through the trees. I whizzed back to Bentley as fast as my paws would carry me.

"B-Bentley." I quivered and pointed to the woods. "I think there's a wolf looking at us."

Before he could reply, there was a movement, and the thing that had been watching us stepped out from the trees into the clearing.

It wasn't a wolf.

This thing was a cat. A Big Cat with sharply curving fangs and more muscles than a couple of weightlifters. Along its flank was a strange logo cut into its fur in the shape of two intertwined letter *K*s. The tiger growled at us again, and I felt my legs weaken. It was the first time I had ever felt that way in front of a cat, and I didn't like it one bit.

Bentley flicked a button on the side of his shades. "'Puter says it's a Siberian tiger. A member of the *Panthera tigris* family. They grow to a maximum of twelve feet long and are shy, nocturnal creatures who are rarely aggressive except when hunting. Says here they're an endangered species."

"Thanks for the wildlife tips," I replied. "Makes me feel so much better about getting eaten. And, for the record, there's only one endangered species around here, and it doesn't look like it's gonna be the tigers."

"Sorry, brother," said the Reverend. "Just wanted you to know what we are up against."

"I know," I said weakly. I made an effort to be upbeat. "Look on the bright side — things can't get any worse."

Then things got worse.

Behind the first cat, a second emerged and stood looking at us like we were mice. Probably confused by the squeaking noises I was making.

"Canine comrades," purred one of the cats in a deep, husky growl. "You are a long vay from home, yes?"

"Keep very still, dude," said Bentley. "Don't make any sudden movements. The slightest sign that we are scared and they'll be after us . . ."

I didn't quite catch the rest of what he said, as I had set off across the snow like a greyhound with its tail on fire as soon as I'd seen the second Siberian tiger. It took Bentley a moment to realize he was on his own.

"We can take 'em!" yelled Bentley. "They're just a coupla cats!"

"Help yourself!" I yelled back. "Me, I'm sticking with this running-fast plan!"

There was a snort of disgust from Bentley, but it didn't take him long to start running. The Siberian tigers were lolloping across the snow towards us.

"I don't care how big they are, it don't feel right being chased by no cat!" he yelled as he caught up with me. (He must have been quite a sprinter to do that, as I was sure that I was breaking the land-speed record for a dog of my size, age, and level of cowardice.)

I felt exactly the same about running from a couple of cats (even if they were the size of a pair of rhinos) but I know my limitations.

As fast as we were running, it was obvious that the Siberian tigers could catch us at any moment. Just as I'd formed this comforting thought, Bentley stopped dead at the top of a rise in the ground.

"What are you doing?" I yelled as I slid to a halt beside him.

Bentley pointed. About five yards in front of us stood a third Siberian tiger. If anything, the new arrival was bigger than the other two. We were trapped. The three tigers slowly began to advance on us. In desperation I pressed the antigravity device on my collar but nothing happened. I did the same with the invisibility button, the rocket-launchers, the shark-repellent, and even the coffee machine, but all were dead as dinosaur droppings.

"Flat battery," said Bentley, pressing all the buttons on his collar. "Nothing's working."

The tigers were so close now that I could smell their breath, and to be honest they could have used some dental hygiene.

"I zink you have novhere else to go, komrades," purred one of the big cats.

"Ach," added the second. "Iss pity. I am feeling not zo 'ungry right now as ve 'ave yust finished our zupper. Hindquarters of a donkey followed by zome verrrry agreeable yak'sh blood."

"Sounds delish." I smirked. "And very filling. Now what was all that about not being hungry?"

"Make no miztake, komrade, ve vill eat you," replied the first cat, just as I was getting my hopes up. "You are yust little dogs, after all."

He smiled lazily and I saw they were preparing to spring, their powerful leg muscles tensing.

Bentley looked at me and I knew what he was thinking. We had been in tough situations before and always managed to think of something. This time we were stumped. It looked like we were going to be dessert.

Bentley cocked a paw and gave me one final salute before our certain and no doubt painful deaths. "It's been a privilege, soldier," he said, his voice all hoarse and broken.

We waited for the tigers to jump. Bentley took up a martial arts stance.

"I'm gonna take at least one of these suckers with me, brother," he hissed through clenched teeth. I adopted a martial arts stance, too, although all I knew about kung fu was from watching late-night movies.

There was something wrong, though. I had closed my eyes tightly, but when I opened them, instead of my flesh being stripped from my bones by the razor-sharp teeth of three ravenous (OK, slightly hungry) Siberian tigers, we were rising slowly into the air. The tigers stood on the snow below, looking at us in puzzlement.

"Yerry strange, komrade," said one of them.

"I agree, komrade," said another. "Iss zome kind of decadent Vestern trickski, I am zinking."

"You are zinking?" said the third. "You must stand on zome firmer ground, zen! Hur hur hur. My joke you are liking, yess?"

I wasn't listening to the triple-act cats. I was too busy celebrating not being dead.

"The collars must be working!" I yelled, happy as a lottery winner.

Bentley shook his head and pointed upwards. For a moment I wondered if the Reverend had pulled a few strings and got The Big Guy working to save our skinny canine behinds. Then I looked up.

A black shape hovered above us. A helicopter. Slowly but surely we rose upwards towards it, pulled in by some sort of tractor-beam gizmo.

Less than a minute later we were inside the CIA chopper, heading back to HQ across the frozen tundra.

Agent 4 was behind the controls, and as I climbed aboard I caught the faintest whiff of . . . of . . . no, it had to be my imagination. For a moment I thought I had picked up the stench of cat. I shook my head and forgot all about it.

Agent 4 was looking down at the flames leaping up from the forklift we'd totaled back at the compound. He didn't look pleased with our handiwork.

"How'd you get to us?" asked Bentley.

"The tracking devices," said Agent 4. "We monitored your mission via satellite and decided to step in. We weren't too concerned about you, but I suppose it's just about possible you may have discovered something useful."

"Gee," I said. "Thanks."

CHAPTER 6

DOG FOOD IS FOREVER

"That's it?" said Agent 4. "A major CIA operation and we end up with . . . that?"

He pointed at the blackened and dented can of doggy chow I'd snagged from the compound. I'd stored it in the pocket of my snazzy snowsuit after it landed next to me in the snow. You never knew when a can of dog food would come in handy.

Agent 4 had asked what we had to show for our

efforts, and the can was all I could produce. It wasn't impressing him.

"Perhaps we should rethink our recruitment policy," he said nastily.

Bentley hoisted himself to his full height, a grim expression on his face.

"Perhaps it's us who should have a rethink, brother," he said. "About joining this two-bit, low-down, backward-lookin', country-boy outfit, if this is all the thanks we get for opening up one real big can of worms. And don't forget, we weren't exactly volunteers for this operation."

Agent 4 smirked.

"Really?"

"Yeah, *really*," said Bentley. "You guys might have a bunch of fancy tricks and plenty of hardware but you can't see what's staring you right in the face. One: That can of dog chow ain't no ordinary can, otherwise why would anyone go to all that trouble to guard the factory like they was makin' gold? Two: Why put a big ole factory down in Siberia if it was strictly on the level? Three: We may be a coupla dumb pooches from the wrong side of the tracks, but even we could see there was something screwy about that lab, with all those bald dogs acting like they got out of bed on the wrong side. As my old mama used to say: If it don't smell right, it don't look right, and if it don't feel right, it probably *ain't* right."

"I couldn't agree with you more, Reverend," said Mr. Smith, opening the door to the briefing room and snatching the can from Agent 4's paw.

"Why wasn't I told they had returned?" he said, looking at Agent 4.

"I was debriefing them in preparation," said Agent 4, shiftily. "Sir."

Mr. Smith paused a long time, looking at Agent 4, before picking up the can again and examining it closely. He tossed it to a nearby agent behind a computer.

"Run a complete system check on this," he barked.

"Run this against the database. Check those letters against all known company logos." He pointed at a scrap of the label that hadn't been burned in the explosion.

"Do you two have anything else from the mission?" asked Mr. Smith, turning to face us.

Bentley stepped forward and fiddled with his shades once more. A beam of light shot out and projected a photograph onto the wall of CIA HQ. It was taken at the factory and showed the fat guy, his cat, and the man with the metal teeth.

"This any use?" said Bentley.

"Hey," I said to the Reverend, "good camera action!"

"This proves nothing," said Agent 4. "This man could be anyone. We'll need more than a photograph and a burned can of dog food to get anywhere with this."

I was about to say something when the agent with the can piped up.

"Sir," he said to Mr. Smith, "I think we have something."

There was a click from the computer and a bright-gold logo flashed up.

"Do we have anything visual on Kreemy Kat?" said Mr. Smith to the dog at the keyboard.

It took just a few seconds to track down a photo of the owner of Kreemy Kat. And hey, guess what?

When the photo flashed up onscreen it was none other than that same fat dude we'd seen back at the Siberian canning factory — the same one Bentley had snapped. On this photo he was sitting on the deck of a boat. He had that skinny cat on his lap and old Iron Gob was standing in the background, looking all fierce.

"Our research has found that the man in the photograph is Dr. Kurt Kreem," said Mr. Smith as we sat in the darkened CIA debriefing room a short time later. He opened a file in front of him and tapped it as he spoke. A photo of the guy from Siberia was projected up onto the wall.

"Kreem, or, as he's sometimes called, 'Fat Kat,' owns one hundred percent of Kreemy Kat Incorporated. Last year they made over five billion dollars from cat food, cat treats, cat baskets, and all other feline-related products."

I whistled.

"You need a whole lot of kitties to make that kind of dough. Five *billion*. Sheesh!"

"Kreem is the best-known cat-lover in the world," continued Mr. Smith. "He's clean as a whistle, as far as we know, although we suspect that somehow a large chunk of Kreem's money has found its way to Cat's Whisker, a feline pressure group that believes in the removal of all dogs from the face of the earth."

"Hey!" I said. "That includes me!"

Mr. Smith nodded. "Of course, we have no proof that Kreem knew he was giving money to Cat's Whisker. They use a lot of regular human charities as a front. For all we know, he may just be one of those weird humans who prefers cats to dogs. Whatever the truth, Kreem definitely needs investigating."

He picked up his pointer and tapped it on Iron Gob.

"This is Kevin Kliche, Kreem's trusted second in command. He's ex-Special Forces, been around, an expert in unarmed and armed combat, a former member of the French Foreign Legion — he was thrown out for being too tough. This is one *bad* apple."

"What's with all the mouth metal?" Bentley asked.

"Kliche has a sweet tooth. His own teeth fell out and he had them replaced with a set of reinforced titanium ones."

Mr. Smith pointed at the cat on Kreem's lap.

"Kissy Karamba, Kreem's latest pet cat. We don't know much about her, except that she starts showing up in photographs with Kreem around a year ago. He's never been seen without her since."

Mr. Smith nodded to whoever was operating the lights and the room brightened. He leaned forward, rested his paws on the table, and continued talking.

"Based on recent events in Siberia, and given Kreem's history, we think it's worth checking him out further. We need some solid information that Kreem is involved in something shady. Which is where you two come in. We want you to make contact with him and see what you can pick up. Why the strange behavior from the dogs? What, if anything, is he planning? You made some good progress in Siberia."

There was what sounded like a laugh from somewhere over in the direction of Agent 4. Mr. Smith ignored him and carried on. "You two are booked on the next available flight to where we believe

Kreem is headed right now — Monte Carlo. He's due to attend a big fundraising cat charity event at the casino."

I couldn't resist a smile. Monte Carlo! Playground of the rich and famous. Glamorous, chic, exotic. Those French poodles! Ooh-la-la!

Mr. Smith brought me back down to earth.

"Of course, this all has to be extremely hush-hush, understand? Keep everything very quiet."

"Of course," I said. "Quiet is my middle name."

I didn't react to Bentley's stifled laugh. It was beneath my dignity.

CHAPTER 7

CASINO ROYALE

"That is one big boat," I said as I lowered the hand-crafted Zeiss triple-lens binoculars. I was looking out of the window of our room at Le Grandiose, the biggest and swankiest hotel in Monte Carlo. I took another look. There it was, bobbing gently at anchor in the marina among all the other rich guys' toys, Kurt Kreem's gleaming white mega-yacht *Thunderpuss*.

"I ain't sure this is going to work," said Bentley from behind me.

I turned and patted his diamond-studded collar.

"Trust me, you look like a million dollars," I said, lying through my teeth; the guy looked beyond ridiculous. "Besides, orders is orders."

Bentley gave a disgusted grunt and regarded his reflection in the mirror. He wasn't happy with what he saw. A CIA hairdresser had styled the fur on his head into a perky pompadour, through which was laced a pink ribbon. The diamond collar and a thorough manicure completed the picture. Bentley now looked every inch the pet of some rich Monte Carlo playboy — apart from looking very much like a heavyweight boxer would appear wearing makeup and a tutu.

If the change in the Reverend's appearance was dramatic, it was nothing compared with what had happened to me. I had spent twelve hours in the CIA lab getting into a rubber-and-metal suit for my transformation from Bad Dog into Bowser Turnberry, international playboy, jetsetter . . . human.

That's right, yours truly had been transformed into a two-legger, right down to robotic fingers and toes. My height had been increased by a complicated set of computerized stilts under my perfectly tailored tuxedo. True, I walked like Frankenstein's monster after a couple of turns on a roller coaster at first, but it improved and the limp that was left could be passed off as a sporting injury. It had been my idea to bring Bentley along as a pet.

"Kreem's got a pet," I said. "It'd look bad if I didn't have one, too. Besides, it means that you can hear all the action."

It had only taken a couple of hours to persuade Bentley to see things my way, and eventually all the preparations were complete. At eight o'clock on the button we strolled through the grand, marble-clad entrance to the casino at Monte Carlo. Maybe "strolled" was exaggerating a bit. "Lurched" might be closer to the truth. I was still getting the hang of this two-legged stuff.

The doorman to the casino gave us a strange look.

"Monsieur," he said, opening the door, "you know zat ziss iss *une soirée de chat*? A cat party?"

"No need to worry, old bean, what what?" I

said to reassure him. "Twinkles here is perfectly trained."

"*Old bean?*" said Bentley. "You're getting carried away with yourself, brother. And less of the *Twinkles* stuff, kapeesh?"

I should mention that Mr. Don't had given me a whizzbang human voice synthesizer gizmo that enabled me to speak human. The human words sounded weird in my head but they seemed good enough for the doorman because he waved us through with a small salute. Bentley (and this was funny) trotted behind me on a leash.

"Heel, boy," I said.

"Don't push it," snarled Bentley.

"Just making everything look convincing," I whispered, but I could tell that the Reverend wasn't convinced in the slightest.

Once inside we made our way to the central room of the casino, where all the bigshots were gathered. There were banners draped across the room advertising the cat charity. I sneered in disgust. What kind of idiots would give money to *cats* when there are perfectly good doggy charities all over the place?

Most people in the casino were gathered around one table, so we hightailed it in that direction. I barged my way through the crowd and suddenly found myself face-to-face with the Man himself: Dr. Kurt Kreem.

He looked up as I squeezed into a seat at the table and I remember thinking that there was something spookily familiar about his smell — but I reckoned that since I was inside the rubber human-suit, my nose was acting up.

Kreem was wedged in his seat with a huge pile of chips in front of him — Doritos, I think, ha ha. On Kreem's lap sat Kissy Karamba, his loathsome pet. All my anti-cat feelings came bubbling to the surface and the old red mist came down in a rush of doggy anger. Karamba bristled at my approach, and I got a feeling that my disguise wasn't going to cut it, as far as she was concerned. Without thinking about what I was doing, I dropped to all fours and snarled at her.

"GRRRRRROWWWWWFFF!" I barked, which, loosely translated, means, "What are you doing here, you repulsive feline?" Then I suddenly remembered I wasn't supposed to be a dog. I got up and laughed it off as best I could, although I couldn't help but notice a few of the customers backed away from me pretty quickly.

"Ah," said Kreem, dusting a couple of pounds of crumbs off his lips. "A joker, I see. Sit down, please Mr. . . . ?"

"Shumbesshy. Fowesher Shumbessy," I blurted out. My talking gizmo was acting up, and I gave the side of my head a whack with the heel of my rubber hand. "Turnberry, I mean. Bowser Turnberry," I said. That was better.

Kreem shifted his bulk and smiled nastily at me. "*Bowser.* Of course."

I leaned across and shook paws — I mean hands — with Kreem.

"Tell me, Mr. 'Turnberry,'" he said, "do you like to play?"

"Yeah!" I said, "Chasing sticks, playing dead . . . I mean, sure, I like to play." Darn it. I'd have to work harder at this human disguise. Behind Kreem, his assistant, Kliche, cracked his knuckles in a meaningful way. Bentley growled at him.

"Bad dog!" I said, tutting at Bentley. "Growling at the nice man with the metal teeth! That's no way to behave, is it?"

Bentley looked at me in a way that would normally have spelled a future of pain for the receiver but, what the heck, I figured this might be my only opportunity to have a bit of fun at the Reverend's expense.

"Pets," I said to Kreem. "What can you do?"

Kreem said nothing for the moment. Kissy Karamba was still bristling at me as Kreem stroked her fur. "Hush, my precious," he said.

I figured he probably wasn't talking to me.

"What's it to be, Mr. Turnberry? A little baccarat perhaps? Or is roulette more to your taste?" he said. "Your choice. And of course winner takes all."

I looked around at the casino. "Tell you what, old bean," I said. "I've got a better idea."

Kreem and I faced each other across a small, round, green felt table. We had been playing for almost twenty minutes and the atmosphere was electric as the game neared a climax.

The crowd had followed us, eager to see this battle of the titans. Kreem had staked his entire stack of chips (the money ones) against mine (CIA had provided me with a stack).

"Your move, I believe, Mr. Turnberry — or should I call you Bowser?"

"Turnberry will do just fine," I said. "Only my friends call me Bowser."

Icy, or what?

I turned back and concentrated on the game of KerPlunk. Gently I reached forward with my plastic hand towards the straws. I selected one and there was a soft gasp from the crowd as the marble teetered on the brink of falling. I could hear Kreem's heavy breathing and the clack of Kliche's metallic teeth. I raised a quizzical eyebrow at Kreem before smiling and confidently whipping the straw free of its hole. There was a moment's silence and then applause as the marble stayed put.

"The old Lin-Chow technique," I said. "Learned it from the KerPlunk Grandmaster himself."

My KerPlunk skills had been finely tuned during a three-month period spent sleeping in the warehouse at Toys "R" Us store in Pasadena, where I'd struck up a friendship with a KerPlunk-playing man named Lin-Chow.

Kreem stared at the remaining straw in disbelief. Kissy Karamba hissed at me in pure hatred. Kreem reached forward and savagely yanked the last straw free. The marble clattered down into his tray. The game was over.

"Congratulations," hissed Kreem, wobbling free of his chair. "This time you win, Mr. Turnberry. Perhaps next time you won't be so . . . fortunate."

I was just trying to come up with a real snappy reply when Bentley tapped me on the leg. I looked down.

"What?"

He pointed to the top of my head. Puzzled, I shot a quick glance at one of the huge gilt mirrors that lined the casino walls. I saw the problem immediately: My head was melting. Under the hot lights my plastic makeup had begun to fall apart. If I didn't do something soon, I'd start to look like a hairy ice-cream cone in July.

To make matters worse, Kreem's repulsive cat looked like she was getting suspicious.

"I'm on to you, bud," she hissed.

And with that she produced a live scorpion (yes, you read that right: A LIVE SCORPION) and casually dropped it down the front of my pants. I wasn't too sure where she'd gotten a scorpion from, but just at that moment Kissy Karamba's spider-hunting techniques weren't exactly on top of my priority list.

There was a short moment of silence when I caught Bentley's eye, and I could tell that he hadn't spotted Karamba's sneaky scorpion-down-the-pants trick. Neither had anyone else, it seemed. Cats, eh? Sly little scuzzballs, every one of them.

Then all thoughts of cats and casinos faded as the scorpion nestled into a more comfortable position from which to sink its fangs or pincers or claws, or whatever fiendish things scorpions have, into my soft parts.

"NEEEEEEEEEEEAAAAAAAAAAAAAARRRRRRR-GGGGGGHHHHHH!!!" I yelled and leaped about eight feet in the air, scissoring my legs as I did so. I twitched and bounced off a large chandelier and fell into an enormous woman in a purple dress. She screamed and heaved me off of her. I tried to apologize but the scorpion made a fresh move somewhere south of my underwear, and I tried to dislodge the little sucker by means of some advanced twisting techniques.

By now I was in the middle of the ballroom, where a large crowd of dancers slowly made room for me. I twirled and swirled. I dropped to my knees, I did backflips, I walked on my hands to try and shake the thing loose. The only thing I didn't do was take off my pants. This wasn't because I was shy, you under-stand, it was because in all the panic caused by the scorpion I had forgotten that this was an option. Plus if I'd taken off my pants I would have let slip that I wasn't Bowser Turnberry.

So I continued to spin around the ballroom like some demented breakdancer. I couldn't keep this up much longer. Sooner or later I was going to get a nasty nip in the lower regions.

There was only one thing to do. I was going to have to kill the scorpion, and I could only think of one way to do it. (Don't forget, I was panicking.)

I raced across the ballroom, ran up the front of a surprised-looking spectator, and flipped high into the air, aided by my special CIA legs. There was a gasp from the crowd as I seemed to hover in midair for a second. Then I dropped to the ballroom floor, my legs in a split position. There was a sickening *pop* as the scorpion bit the dust (although thankfully nothing else).

The crowd went berserk and a small chubby guy dressed in a spangly suit came forward and presented me with a large silver trophy. MONTE CARLO FELINE FRIENDS CHARITY EVENT OPEN DISCO DANCE COMPETITION WINNER read the inscription.

"Congratulations!" said the guy. "Zat was zimply magnificent, monsieur!"

I was about to say something when his eye caught my melting head.

"Monsieur! Your 'ead! You 'ave damaged yourself I zink! We must get *un docteur!*"

He began to wave his arms around and create quite a fuss, and I could see my cover was in danger of being well and truly blown.

Just then Bentley raced through the crowd, grabbed hold of my ankle between his teeth, and dragged me out of the ballroom, across the casino floor and down the steps, my rubber head bouncing off each one as we made our escape. Just ahead of us, Kreem, Kliche, and Kissy Karamba were getting into a large white limousine. The cat spotted us and gave me a nasty little smile.

Bentley dragged me around the corner and let go of my ankle.

"Very cool," he said. "You just blended right in there. Any plans to defend your disco-dance trophy next year? Or are you going to quit while you're still at the top?"

I figured he was probably being sarcastic.

"You try looking cool with a live scorpion down your shorts," I replied. "Let me tell you, it isn't easy."

I explained what had happened with Karamba, and even Bentley had to admit I had a point.

"Man, that sucks," he said with feeling. "I didn't think even a cat would sink that low. By the way, you're beginning to freak me out a little, brother. You look like something from a horror movie."

I began to peel off my disguise.

"So what now?" I said as I scooped a handful of melted nose off my ear.

Bentley narrowed his eyes and looked mean. The effect was spoiled a little by the curly pink ribbon, but he still looked like someone you'd cross the road to avoid.

"Let's check out his boat," he said, and pointed towards the marina.

CHAPTER 8

DIAMONDS ARE FOREVER

I felt a lot more comfortable when I had gotten out of all that human makeup and clothing and was once more my gorgeous doggy self. I don't know how the two-leggers can stand having all that extra stuff hanging off 'em, all those clothes and glasses and hair. Me, I prefer life as a nudist. I'd like to have kept the disco-dancing trophy, though. As it was, the Reverend made me stash it in a bush.

Ten minutes after leaving the casino we were dockside at the swanky marina, about a hundred yards away from the *Thunderpuss,* hiding behind some garbage cans. Bentley and I had formed a cunning plan and Bentley was arguing about part of it.

"I don't see why we can't just walk up to the boat and look through the window," he said.

"We already went through this, Reverend," I said, patiently. "One: The boat is not tied up at the jetty, it's too big. Two: Kreem has security guys on the dock closest to the boat. Three: In all the spy movies there's a part where they swim up to the bad guy's boat. OK?"

"But you know I can't swim," said Bentley. This was true. He had been arguing furiously about this part of the plan all the way down to the marina.

"A detail. All dogs can swim. That's why they call it the doggy-paddle, right? Besides," I said, stifling a snicker, "those things kind of suit you. No offense."

I pointed at the flowery-patterned orange water wings the Reverend had lifted from one of the yachts and insisted on wearing.

"None taken, brother." Bentley grunted and cuffed me gently with a piece of wood he'd found next to the garbage cans.

"OK, OK!" I said, rubbing a lump the size of a squirrel that had mysteriously sprung up on the side of my head. "I won't mention the water w —"

I tailed off as Bentley eyed the piece of wood again. Sheesh, some people are so touchy.

"Remember," I said as I slipped into the inky-black water, "this plan depends on absolute silence."

Bentley nodded and leaped into the water. There was a splash that could have been heard back in Vladivostok.

"Or we could just abandon the absolute silence part and let them know we're on our way," I said bitterly, under my breath (I didn't want another whomp from the Reverend's piece of wood).

I looked across to *Thunderpuss* expecting to see guards appearing at the rails, but it looked as though no one had heard. We paddled across to the side of the yacht, which looked even bigger up close. Right away Bentley spotted a ladder leading up to the deck and bobbed over to it as fast as his little water wings would carry him. We hoisted ourselves aboard and crept behind a large storage locker to catch our breath. Out of curiosity I peeked inside and nearly fell over. The locker was chock-full of diamonds. Big, shiny, proper, in-your-face diamonds.

"Check this out!" I gasped.

The Reverend peeked over the lid and raised one eyebrow. That meant he was really excited.

"What do you think?" I said. "Is this just what rich guys have at their parties instead of bowls of nuts?"

Bentley picked up one of the diamonds and looked at it carefully.

"These sparklers are industrial diamonds," he said. "The kind they use in cutting tools, or drills, or lasers."

"Lasers? What's a cat-food manufacturer doing messing around with lasers?"

We didn't have time to think about this, as a crew member came around the corner and we had to duck down as he passed. I scooped up a bucketful of diamonds and stowed them in a handy sack I found nearby.

From the main cabin directly in front of us came  the muffled sound of the ship's crew preparing a dinner party for Kreem when he returned from the casino. They were probably hoisting a full-size roast pig onto the table right now.

"Let's see what else we can find," I said, and we slipped along the deck, keeping an eye out for guards or any spare Siberian tigers Kreem might have brought along for the ride. I was inching towards the cabin window when a piercing canine howl cut through the Monte Carlo night. It was hideous. It sounded like someone had tried to hurdle a razor-wire fence and misjudged it by a few inches.

"Oh sweet Lord," said the Reverend. "We have got to help that poor tormented hound."

I nodded in agreement as another teeth-juddering screech ripped through the space between my ears. What unspeakable torture was going on in that cabin?

We moved closer and then stopped as most of the room came into view. There were half a dozen cabin crew busying themselves around the table. They were paying no attention whatsoever to the noise coming from over by the piano.

"That sound!" I gasped. "I can't stand it! We gotta do something, Bentley!"

Bentley nodded, his face like thunder. He looked around and spotted a fire extinguisher on one wall next to a panel marked *Fuses*. He ripped the extinguisher off and looked at me. "We gotta stop this, right?"

I nodded.

"We go in, we grab that poor dog, and we take him back to HQ, OK?"

I nodded again. This torture had to be stopped

somehow. Agent 4 was going to have a fit, but he wasn't here to witness what was going on. I knew one thing: I couldn't sit here and listen to that for much longer. Our secret mission would have to go public.

Bentley yanked open the fusebox just as a guy wearing white came round the corner. It was one of Kreem's crew.

"Hey!" he shouted as Bentley smashed the butt-end of the extinguisher into the fusebox. Instantly all the lights went out onboard the *Thunderpuss*. Thankfully the screaming from inside the cabin had stopped, too, and we burst through the doors.

Inside it was black. I lost track of exactly where everything was, although I could just make out Bentley's orange water wings as he blundered around looking for the dog who was in pain. The room echoed to the sound of grunts, thuds, crashes, and shouting as the crew bounced off Bentley. Glasses tinkled to the floor and furniture cracked as everyone struggled in the blackness.

"Fix those lights!" shouted a voice.

"I got him!" I yelled, groping a squishy human shape. "Oops, my mis-take, madam."

I scrambled off the large waitress and bumped into another shape, which lay shivering on the floor. I reached down and my paw touched its trembling fur.

"Don't worry," I said. "We're here to rescue you!"

The dog made no response. I figured it was in shock.

"Over here!" I shouted to the Reverend.

Bentley's Day-Glo arms raced across the cabin. He scooped up the dog and shoved him into the sack of diamonds and yanked it shut.

"Sorry 'bout that, brother," said Bentley, patting the sack. "But you're probably safer in there until we get you outta here."

Pumped up with excitement and anger over the treatment of one of our own, we crashed through the cabin doors and vaulted over the railings into the water. Bullets zipped past our ears and we doggy-paddled like maniacs for the shore.

The lights came back on aboard the *Thunderpuss* and a spotlight swept across the marina. I pulled Bentley underwater and kicked hard for the jetty. A few moments later we reached the wooden ladder and hoisted ourselves up and behind the garbage cans again. The sack containing the dog had gone very still.

Back on land, things were far from quiet. The garbage cans pinged and rocked as bullets bounced off them.

"We've got to get out of here!" I yelled to Bentley and pressed the emergency rescue button on the side of my spy collar. Almost at once the sky was full of noise as a CIA RRU (Rapid Response Unit) heli-copter swept low across the marina and plucked us off the dock.

I lay back, wet, exhausted, and happy, against the side of the chopper. A large bullmastiff in a black combat suit shook me by the paw.

"YOU OK, SOLDIER?" he barked in a deep voice over the roar of the helicopter rotor blades.

I nodded.

"GOOD WORK!" he shouted and moved back to the cockpit. The pilot, a "been-there-done-that" chi-huahua with a long scar down one side of his face, gave us the paws-up as we settled back for the ride to HQ.

"Feels good, don't it?" I smiled at Bentley. "Striking a blow for dogs everywhere, keeping the canine world safe — what?"

This last bit was in response to Bentley's face. It had that "not again" look on it.

He patted the wet sack containing the rescued dog.

"Just exactly *how* sure are you that we got a dog inside here?"

"I'm sure, I'm sure," I said. "It was the poor guy all right, all trembly and furry. You don't think I'd make a mistake about something as important as that, do you?"

Bentley didn't reply. He just opened the sack and looked inside.

"See?" I said. "We got him, right? I knew all alo —" I tailed off as Bentley reached inside the sack and lifted out a dripping human wearing a furry coat and baggy pants.

"Please don't hurt me," it said. "Let me stay on my own planet."

CHAPTER 9

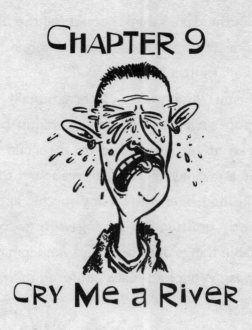

CRY ME A RIVER

"In ten years in the service I've never seen anything quite so stupid, so . . . so . . ."

Agent 4 couldn't finish. His face was contorted in fury as he paced back and forth in front of us.

"Your mission was to get information about Kreem, not to kidnap a respectable member of the human race! You couldn't even get your 'rescue' right, could you?"

"Easy mistake to make," I muttered. "It was dark."

"Even in the dark I think I could tell the difference between a tortured dog and someone like Mr. Jimberlake!" ranted Agent 4.

Mr. Tustin Jimberlake. Internationally famous human pop singer and all-around pinup boy. He'd been hired at huge expense to entertain Kreem's guests at a swanky dinner party aboard the yacht. Jimberlake had been rehearsing for his appearance when we'd confused his singing with a dog having unspeakable things done to it and yanked him off the *Thunderpuss*. What had really confused us was his fur

coat. (Turned out to be fake fur, too, as Jimberlake was a *vegetarian*, if you can believe such things exist.) It was him we had accidentally kidnapped and dragged back to CIA headquarters. He was sitting in one corner trembling as he watched us dogs yakking away.

"Look at him!" snapped Agent 4. "He thinks he's been abducted by aliens who resemble dogs. We're going to have to do a full memory wipe on him. He'll probably never sing again."

"At least some good's come out of all this then," I quipped, but it didn't even raise a smile.

"It's a complete fiasco," continued Agent 4.

"I still think there's something not right about that dude," said Bentley, nodding in the direction of Tustin Jimberlake. "The way he was howling, he's got to have a little bit of cat mixed up in there somewhere. And even if he is alright, what about Kreem? What about those diamonds? And we still haven't gotten to the bottom of that weird Siberian factory."

Just then the door opened and Mr. Smith trotted in. Agent 4 brought him up to speed about our little trip, making sure that we came out of it looking bad.

Mr. Smith turned to face us, a sour look on his face.

"This doesn't sound good, gentlemen. Bringing a human back to HQ is strictly against our code. We have the Utah Center for dealing with humans. Agent 4 here is keen to send you back to Z-Block, and it'd be no more than you foul-ups deserve."

Mr. Smith paused and I sat up, all ears now. Back to Z-Block?

"However," he continued, "I kind of like your style. We should have been alerted to Kreem some time ago." He broke off and shot a look at Agent 4, then continued, "And I do think you may have a point about Dr. Kreem . . ."

Bentley gave him a bitter smile. Agent 4 looked as though he was about to explode.

". . . and with that in mind, I've decided to give you one more try. This time, though, you'll be on your own. No support from us, no RRUs, no backup of any kind. If you mess up, then we don't want to know. We simply cannot afford another human crossover like this one, understand? We'll drop you at Kreem's location — our agents are tracking his yacht as we speak — but then it's up to you. Your mission is to collect evidence of Kreem's involvement. On no account are you to reveal yourselves or the CIA in any way. Is that clear?"

Bentley and I nodded slowly. Anything was better than going back on the block. And now I wanted to nail Kreem and his revolting cat. It was getting personal after that scorpion incident.

"And if we do get Kreem for whatever it is he's doing?" said Bentley.

Mr. Smith smiled wolfishly. "Then of course we'll take the credit. But at least you get the satisfaction of knowing you served the doggy nation, right? Now get out of my sight."

All warmth and heart, that guy.

Four days later we were booted out of another CIA plane somewhere over the Pacific Ocean. We drifted down towards Kreem's secret tropical island lair, which is where the yacht had gone after leaving Monte Carlo.

We splashed down gently in the shallow waters about two hundred yards from the beach. Bentley was a little more confident in the water but still wore his Day-Glo water wings. We wasted no time ditching our 'chutes, as the CIA agents had helpfully told us they'd discovered that Kreem kept the island surrounded by man-eating sharks.

"Seeing as you two are dogs, that *might* not be a problem," one of them had said as he booted me out of the plane.

In fact almost as soon as I'd surfaced I caught sight of a fin cutting through the water towards me. In an instant I had formed a plan to drag Bentley in front of me and offer him up as a snack while I made it to shore. Unfortunately, blind panic took over and I screamed like a pup.

"SHARK!" I yelled.

Something bumped my leg below the water and I fainted. When I came to, we were being carried towards the beach on the backs of a couple of friendly, playful dolphins.

"'Sharks,'" said Bentley in disgust. "Can't you tell the difference between a shark and a dolphin, brother?"

"Listen," I said in a low voice, "as far as I'm concerned, a dolphin's just a shark in a smart suit. This thing nearly took my leg off back there."

"Dolphins don't eat dogs," said Bentley confidently.

"They could be sharks in disguise," I said.

"Then why are they helping us get to the beach?"

Bentley had a point, so I shut up.

The dolphins dropped us off in the shallows near to the beach and swam away. I swear that one of them saluted.

We took no chances on the dolphins/sharks changing their diet and made it onto the beach in under twenty seconds — a new world record for the doggy-paddle, I believe. In fact, I was still furiously trying to swim up the beach when Bentley reminded me we were out of the water and therefore probably out of range of any dog-eating dolphins.

"I knew that," I said, standing and brushing the sand off.

We looked around and decided that even though it was still dark, we'd best get undercover. After what we'd seen in Siberia, who knew what security measures Kreem would have in place here? We trotted across to the thick jungle that hugged the beach and tried to get our bearings.

The beach we were on was the only stretch of sand; everywhere else on the island was rocky, or at least that's what the boys back at the CIA had told us. Nestled among the trees was the main building, a long, low, tropical-style luxury island hideaway for Kreem. The big fat lug was probably snoring in there right now.

We headed through the thick vegetation towards the house. It was tough going, all vines and creepers and nasty slithery things, which brushed against you in the dark. Ahead of me on the trail Bentley suddenly stopped and peered hard into the jungle.

"Look!"

He pointed through the trees and I peered into the murk. At first I couldn't see a thing, but after a moment I could make out the edge of a wall. I pricked up my ears and the sound of barking, frantic barking, came from somewhere inside. We scrambled across until we were pushed up against the wall of a long concrete shed with a tin roof, set in a small clearing. An electricity generator hummed away over at one end.

I stood on Bentley to get a look through the window. Inside it was dim but what I could see looked very familiar.

"It's just like the lab he's got in Siberia," I said. "Lots of caged dogs, lots of scientific equipment. What is this guy up to?"

Bentley lowered me down.

"We need information," said Bentley. "I'm gonna ask one of those pooches what the heck is going on."

"Those guys in Siberia weren't too welcoming," I reminded him. "Dogs or no dogs."

"Have faith, brother. I'm gonna make them an offer they can't refuse," he said, smiling grimly. He scuttled down to the doorway and went inside while I kept watch. I heard a series of thumps and soft bangs, then the lab door opened again and Bentley came out holding a baldy dog under his arm.

"This is Pablo," said Bentley. "He has kindly agreed to fill us in on some background information, isn't that right, Pablo?"

Pablo gasped as Bentley gripped his neck tightly.

"*Sí, sí,* señor!" he managed to croak. "I tella you what's goin' on, YOU FILTHY SCUM!"

I looked at him, eyebrows raised.

"Sorry, señor," he said. "We cannot 'elp ourselves from sayin' things like dat, it's just 'I HATE YOU!' pops out even when we don' want it."

"Just like all the dogs in Siberia," I said to Bentley.

"Is the food," said Pablo. "YOU STINK! It is the food they make us eat. It forces you to shout stuff, bite things, act like craz — FILTHY FLEABAG SON OF A PIGDOG!" He twisted and bit Bentley on the arm.

"Hey, brother!" said Bentley.

"Sorry, señor," said Pablo. "I can't help myself, YA BIG WET HEAP OF DONKEY DUNG!"

Just then there was the sound of a bell and Pablo perked up, his little Mexican ears all a-quiver. He started drooling and getting very excited.

"Señor! Señor! Put me down, please. YOU HAVE FLEAS! I must go! Very important!"

Inside the lab all the other dogs were going crazy, too.

"OK, Pablo," I said. "What's the big deal with the bell? Why all the fuss?"

Pablo was wriggling like a fish on a hook.

"Breakfast!" he barked. "Food! Breakfast! Breakfast! I must eat!"

Bentley put Pablo down and he raced back into the lab. We watched through a window as he shot straight back to his cage and pulled the door shut. Then, like all the other pooches, he howled and barked and yelped as though he had a couple of dozen African bees trapped in his rear end.

"Weird," I said. "They don't look hungry."

"They aren't," said Bentley. "Some of those guys are pretty chubby."

A door opened in the lab and in came our old friend Kliche carrying a case of dog food.

"Look!" I whispered. "The same dog food we saw in Siberia."

"Looks to me like they want those dogs to be as nasty as possible," said the Reverend. "That's why old Metal Mouth is feedin' them up."

Kliche ripped open the cans of food with his metal teeth and scooped it out into trays set into the cages. It was immediately gobbled up by all the dogs. Kliche waited until they had finished, then opened a couple of cages and lifted two dogs out. He turned and went back through the door.

"After him!" I said.

We raced into the lab, ignoring the insults from the cages, and slipped through the door after Kliche. Ahead of us, down a long corridor, we could see Kliche turning a corner, a struggling dog under each massive arm. The corridor twisted and turned and it was difficult to keep Kliche in view. Suddenly he stopped and pushed open a huge metal door. From beyond came the soft hum of machinery and the noise of people. I shivered and wondered if we were going deep into some sort of gigantic and mysterious underground lair, where Kreem would be sitting in a big swivel chair in front of a glowing map of the world with his cat on his lap, about to do something really nasty and evil.

There was only one way to find out. We stepped through the heavy metal door.

CHAPTER 10

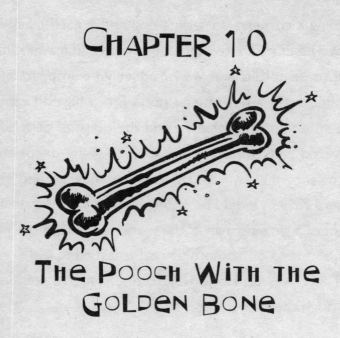

THE POOCH WITH THE GOLDEN BONE

On the other side of the door was a gigantic, mysterious, secret underground lair carved into the mountain under Kreem's house. Along one wall was a glowing map of the earth, in front of which sat Kreem on a large swivel chair. Kissy Karamba sat purring on his lap. Kreem looked like he was about to do something really nasty and evil. Spooky, or what?

In the center of the room was a complicated machine covered in dials and wires, and with a big barrel pointing at the roof. A large sign hung over it saying WARNING: SECRET LASER MACHINE. All around the cavern, men in white coats twiddled with knobs and dials in a meaningful way. Some of them carried clipboards, and here and there stood guards in blue uniforms. We ducked down behind a metal box, which looked like it had been put there just so spies like us could hide behind it.

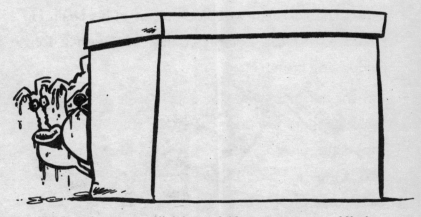

"What kept you?" I heard Kreem snap at Kliche. "You know that timing is everything with these dogs. They must be in perfect condition when we launch."

Kliche just nodded, and I realized that he probably couldn't talk. His teeth must have been too heavy. Kliche handed the two dogs to one of the assistants and went and stood behind Kreem's chair. He did a lot of that, standing behind chairs. Must get boring sometimes, being the chief henchman for an evil genius who wants to take over the world.

Bentley nudged me in the ribs. "Look."

We watched the assistant carry the two dogs towards the Secret Laser Machine. As they approached, Kreem wobbled up out of his chair. He talked to his cat, pointing things out with a long golden dog bone.

"We will not have to wait much longer, my precious," he said, cackling wildly. "Soon my Secret Laser Machine will rid the world of dogs . . . forever! Ha ha ha ha ha!"

I wondered exactly how his Secret Laser Machine was going to do that. Fortunately, Kreem explained.

"Yes, my Secret Laser Machine, which I've been secretly making here at my remote and secret tropical island lair, is almost ready for its final phase! It will make all our other plans seem like, er . . . umm, like plans that didn't work properly. For six months we have been selling Kreemy K-9 Dog Food to all the dog-lovers in the world. Little did those fools suspect I had doctored the revolting stuff with a secret ingredient, one that made all dogs act crazy! Ha ha ha ha!"

This last part was Kreem doing some more cackling. The old ham.

"So that explains all those loopy pooches," I whispered.

"And the secret Siberian dog-food factory," said Bentley.

Kreem continued. "But the plan was too slow, and their hair was falling out too so we began to build this magnificent Secret Laser Machine to speed up my evil scheme. All we have to do now is feed a couple of deranged dogs into the fuel cell, suck their brains dry, and point it at the moon."

"Eh?" I whispered. "How is that going to do anything?"

"Excuse me, Dr. Kreem," said an assistant. "I'm still a bit unsure about how pointing the Secret Laser Machine at the moon and fueling it with the brain fluids from two loopy pooches is going to rid the world of dogs."

"Good question," I said quietly. "And perfectly timed."

Kreem looked at the assistant and pulled a nearby lever. The floor opened up underneath the assistant and he plunged screaming into what was obviously a pit filled with man-eating sharks. Probably the ones we hadn't come across earlier.

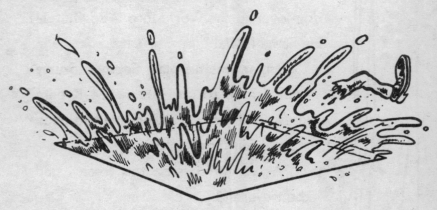

"Fool," said Kreem. "It is simple. The Secret Laser Machine will suck the essence of crazy dog from these two repulsive canines and fire a powerful beam of doggy horribleness at a precise point on the moon. This beam, focused to a perfect pulse of light energy by a lens made from pure South African diamonds" — I nodded to Bentley at the mention of diamonds — "will bounce back and cover most of

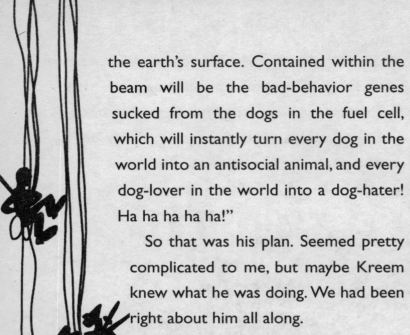

the earth's surface. Contained within the beam will be the bad-behavior genes sucked from the dogs in the fuel cell, which will instantly turn every dog in the world into an antisocial animal, and every dog-lover in the world into a dog-hater! Ha ha ha ha ha!"

So that was his plan. Seemed pretty complicated to me, but maybe Kreem knew what he was doing. We had been right about him all along.

"We've got to stop this freak," said the Reverend.

I was about to form a cunning plan when a whole bunch of ninjas rappelled down from the ceiling and surrounded us. Kreem's voice turned in our direction.

"You can come out from behind those pointless metal boxes, *Mr. Turnberry* and your not-so-little pet," he said. "It is stupid to pretend. We have known all along you were on the island, gentlemen."

Bentley wanted to fight the ninjas, but we were hopelessly outnumbered. We got up from our hiding place and walked out, paws in the air. Kissy Karamba hissed at us, but I couldn't help notice there was something not quite right about her; she seemed distracted, agitated. Perhaps she was feeling bad about dropping that scorpion down my shorts.

We were escorted across to face Kreem. His chubby face beamed smugly as he looked at us.

"I told you that beating me at KerPlunk was just a temporary setback," he said.

"Who's the tattletale?" I asked. "How did you know we were here? Someone musta squealed."

Kreem just laughed.

"Ha ha ha! You mean you do not know, *Mr. Turnberry*? I've been planning for your arrival here for some time."

"Wait a minute," said Bentley. "There's something screwy about this. How come you can understand what we're saying? We ain't wearing any human speech translator."

"You are most observant. It's good to see that at least one of you shows some intelligence. I have known from the very start of this affair exactly where you two numbskulls would be. You could say that I have . . . inside information. And the reason I can understand every word you say is quite simple."

Kreem paused and dropped Kissy Karamba to the floor. She meowed and he casually booted her into a corner as if she was a piece of garbage. This was the first surprise. The second was something else entirely.

We watched in total horror as Kreem reached around the back of his massive head and pulled at something. With a jerky tug he unzipped his head clean down the middle, from the back of his neck to a point about twenty inches below his fifth chin. I almost passed out from shock. When my vision cleared I could see the full horror of what had happened.

Kreem was speaking.

"The reason I can understand you and I know so much about what's going on, Mr. Turnberry, is that I am . . . a dog."

It was true. Inside Kreem's head was indeed a dog. But this wasn't just any old dog. Inside Kreem's head was none other than Agent 4.

He wore a complicated headset with wires running from it down into the rest of Kreem's body. It must have been a bit like the human disguise I wore posing as Bowser Turnberry at the casino. Only this one didn't melt.

"You!" I gasped.

"I never trusted that guy," said Bentley. "Lousy, stinkin' traitor."

Agent 4 smirked.

"But why?" I said. "Why get us to investigate you? And how did you get down onto the island? We just left you in the plane!"

"I picked you because you two are total idiot losers, of course," said Agent 4. "That jumped-up rat Smith was going to investigate the Siberian factory anyway. Little did he know he had placed the very person responsible for the whole thing in charge of the investigation. Naturally I decided the best thing to do was to get them to send a couple of morons. That way they would find out nothing and the case would be closed, leaving me free to continue my mission. Simple. As for getting onto the island, I left CIA HQ two days ago on some excuse and caught a flight down to the islands to prepare for the final phase of my glorious plan!"

We looked at him.

"Those fools at the CIA never recognized my genius," he said. "They were too slow, too tiny-minded to see the big picture. It's a dog-eat-cat world out there, and the cats are winning. They don't need to be walked, they eat less, and they do their business in private on someone else's garden. No wonder the humans are starting to realize that cats are much easier to look after. Soon we'll be second-class pets in our own world! And all the CIA could do was stand by and watch. Not me. I wanted more than they could ever dream of! A world where dogs could rule in complete and total isolation. Once I get rid of most of my fellow pooches, the world will see cats for the miserable creatures they really are, and will destroy them. When that happens, I will replace them with clones of myself. Imagine, an entire doggy planet filled with copies of me! What a glorious future lies ahead for the canine world!"

Agent 4 stood lost in dreams of total doggy domination.

"So let me get this straight," I said. "You want to get rid of all cats by getting rid of all dogs and replacing them with little versions of you?"

Agent 4 nodded.

"Wouldn't it be easier to just get rid of all the cats with the laser?" said Bentley.

Agent 4 looked at us blankly, little red points of light glinting in his eyes. I knew right then he was as mad as a nudist at the North Pole.

"But where's the fun in that?" he said. "Unless a plan is really, really complicated, it's not worth doing. And besides, the world is overrun with mongrel breeds like you two. It is time to start afresh with a glorious new race of pure-bred pedigree perfection!"

"But aren't you, you know, a mongrel?" I asked.

Agent 4 looked like he was going to eat me alive.

"A mongrel?! I am pure-bred! The first of a new breed of superdog!"

I looked at Bentley and made little circular motions with my paw at the side of my head.

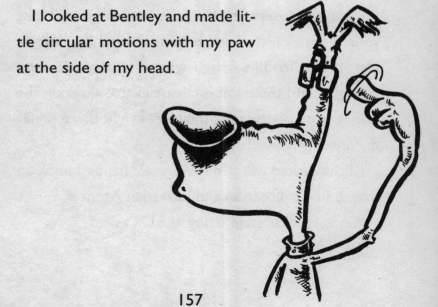

"Uh-huh." He nodded in agreement. "Completely loopy."

"Barking," I said.

Agent 4 looked at us in disgust.

"Enough of this nonsense!" he snapped. "Kliche, put these idiots in the Secret Laser Machine with those other idiots!"

Kliche must have had some kind of dog translation device because he understood every word Kreem was saying.

Agent 4 turned to us, the plastic sides of Kreem's face wobbling in a vomit-induced way.

"You two losers are the lucky ones! You will take your place in history by helping to fuel its magnificent beam! To think that I wasted all this effort on trying to find the dumbest, least likable dogs on the planet when all the time they were right there under my nose!"

Kliche picked us up in his gigantic hands. I jerked a thumb in his direction and looked at Agent 4.

"So is Frankenstein a dog, too?" I asked.

Agent 4 shook his head as he busied himself with the dials on the Secret Laser Machine.

"All too human, I'm afraid," he said. "They have little imagination but do come in handy at times. And he is paid very handsomely for his work."

"What about the cat?" said Bentley. "Is she for real?"

"The cat?" said Agent 4, blankly. "Oh. That. Yes, she is real enough, I think. She was perfect cover for my role as Dr. Kurt Kreem, cat-lover extraordinaire. She is completely repulsive to me, naturally, and she will perish alongside you when the Secret Laser Machine explodes."

"Explodes?" I said. I didn't like the sound of that.

"Why yes," answered Agent 4. "This beam will be so powerful that it can only last for a minute before the machine overheats and explodes in a really big ball of fire, which will destroy everything and everyone on the island. Myself and my assistants will escape using our personal jetpacks. Kliche and the assistants are of no use to me after the beam has done its work and I would prefer to leave them all here, but they insisted on escaping, too. Humans. They have no sense of destiny."

"Do you expect us to let you get away with this?" I said, a little more bravely than I was feeling.

"Why no, Mr. Turnberry," said Agent 4, walking away. "I expect you to die." He stopped at the doorway and turned around. "I've been wanting to say that for *so* long."

CHAPTER 11

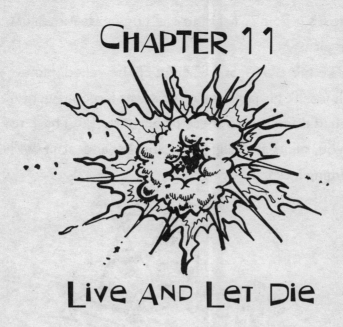

LIVE AND LET DIE

Kliche strapped us into the Secret Laser Machine next to the two other dogs he'd placed inside earlier.

"Just in case," said Agent 4 when I asked why there were going to be four of us pooches strapped into the fuel cell. "Can't take any chances now, not when I am so close! With four of you loser mutts in there, the beam will be super-concentrated!"

"How's it goin'?" I said to the dog nearest me, just to be pleasant.

"BITE MY BUTT, SCUZZFACE!" he yelled. I knew that it wasn't his fault, seeing as it was Kreem/Agent 4 who had done this to these poor mutts, but I have to tell you, all that yelling and insults and stuff was becoming a tad annoying.

"Quiet, you mongrel scum!" screeched Agent 4, which was a bit rich coming from a nonpedigree pooch like himself, even if he did think he was a new breed of superdog or some such waffle.

He and Kliche were strapping themselves into personal jetpacks and preparing to zip away to wherever evil maniacs and their silent henchmen go at this point in the story. The rest of the white-coated assistants and guards all seemed to have slipped away, too, leaving just the main players in the lair. Agent 4 pressed a button and the vast sliding doors in the roof slowly slid apart to reveal the night sky. A full yellow moon hung, fat and round, among the stars. It was a perfect night to get frazzled into tiny bits of carbon by a super-heated Secret Laser Machine and then beamed to the moon to be bounced back to earth to infect the doggy population with an evil virus. I wished it was raining.

"I have set the timer for four minutes," said Agent 4, slipping out of the rest of his Dr. Kreem outfit. "That will give you time to say your goodbyes and reflect upon your fate while we escape, ha ha ha ha ha ha ha ha ha ha ha!"

His laugh was getting on my nerves, and I remembered bitterly that I'd heard it before, back at CIA HQ when we'd been told we were going to Siberia. That laugh alone should have tipped us off that the guy was eleven dimes short of a dollar.

With a whoosh of compressed air, Kliche and Agent 4 rose slowly, Agent 4 cackling like a wild thing.

"Quit the cackling!" yelled the Reverend.

"Goodbye, *Mr. Turnberry*! Goodbye, Reverend Bentley!" shouted Agent 4. "Next stop, the moon!"

And with that they zipped up, up, and away, out through the gap in the cavern's roof and into the wild blue yonder.

Back in the Secret Laser Machine room there was silence, broken only by the colorful cursing coming from our Kreemy-Dog-Food–infected pals. They seemed to think we had something to do with them being strapped into the laser and were busily point-ing out bits of our anatomy they considered unusual, as well as making some very personal comments about our mothers.

"Well," I said to Bentley, "that's another fine mess you've gotten me into."

"Looks that way, brother," said the Rev. "Unless you've got any clever ideas?"

I rummaged around furiously in my brain, poking into long-unused corners and looking under piles of meaningless garbage I had hanging around in there for a way out of this.

"Nope," I said. "Absolutely nothing. You?"

Before Bentley could say anything, there was a cough from a corner of the cavern and something moved.

It was Kissy Karamba.

She slowly got to her paws, rubbing her head, and looked around. Agent 4 had knocked her senseless and she was probably wondering exactly how she had ended up trapped down here on the island with a bunch of dogs. She tootled across to the Secret Laser Machine and looked inside where the four of us lay strapped down.

"Great," I said. "The only thing left alive on the island that can help and it turns out to be a scorpion-wielding psycho cat. Unless you've got a trick or two up your sleeve?"

"Funny you should say that," said Kissy Karamba, fiddling with something on the back of her neck. For a minute I thought she was going to unzip her head, too, but all she did was press a stud on her collar, which triggered some kind of inflatable military uniform to spring out. A headset wrapped itself around her head and various aerials and antennae sprouted from her helmet.

"Is *everyone* not what they seem around here?" said Bentley looking at me. "What about you, brother? You got any little surprises for the Reverend? I mean this whole head-unzipping and disguise thing is gettin' out of control."

"And why are you still around?" I piped up. "Shouldn't you be sneaking off somewhere? Cats! I hate cats!"

"No kidding," said the cat formerly disguised as Kissy Karamba. "Dogs ain't exactly on my 'friends and family' phone list. Now quit yapping."

She unclipped the four of us and stuck out a paw, which I took after a moment's hesitation. This was a cat, after all.

"The name's Kowalski. Agent Charlene Kowalski, Cat's Whisker Special Super-duper Under-undercover Operative. I've been working this case since we first suspected Kreem wasn't the cat-lover he seemed. I was making some progress, although, I got to admit, I never had a CIA agent down as the perp. Caught me cold with that little bombshell. I think it's about time we all joined forces, don't you?"

"Hey," I said, as I remembered something. "If you're a Cat's Whisker agent, and you suspected we were investigating Kreem, too, how come you slipped that spooky scorpion down my shorts? That could have been very nasty! And how did you know I was a dog?"

Kowalski grinned.

"Sorry 'bout the scorpion," she said, "but I had to distract you somehow. I thought you could have been trouble. I knew that if Kreem had found out he was being investigated by someone, he might have started suspecting people closer to home, like me, for example. I didn't know he was already one step ahead of everyone. Besides, it was a Brazilian striped scorpion; it looks nasty but is completely harmless. I always keep a few close to paw in case I need a distraction. And you kind of gave the dog thing away at the casino by barking at me, remember?"

"Oh," I said, "that."

"This is all very interesting, sister," said the Reverend Bentley, interrupting, "and we are *very* grateful to be out of the Secret Laser Machine, but can I remind everyone about the timer? We've only got about a minute left before it explodes, not to mention the beam of dog-destructive virus that'll be heading for the moon."

"Oh, don't worry," said Agent Kowalski. "I always had a fallback plan for that."

She raced across to one of the big metal lockers at one side of the room and pulled out five jet-packs.

"Put these on and . . ."

I didn't hear the rest of what she was saying because I had slapped that jetpack sucker on and blasted away through the gap in the roof in about sixty seconds less than a New York minute. I noticed the other two mutts had done exactly the same and roared past me at a gazillion miles an hour. I must have had a slow one. I waved to them as they passed.

"YOU STINK!" yelled one.

"YOU HAVE A BIG NOSE
AND I HATE YOU!" said the other one.

"And good luck to you, too!" I yelled back. "Have
a nice day!"

I looked down and saw Bentley and Kowalski fiddling with something on the Secret Laser Machine. Then they too blasted off and were soon alongside me.

"Er, I was just checking that the coast was clear for our escape," I said. I didn't want them to get the wrong idea about me clearing off so quickly.

"Hmm," said Bentley in a coolish tone. "Checking. Right."

Just then there was a loud humming noise and the air seemed to vibrate. A beam of blinding light shot past us from the island. It was the laser!

"I thought you had it covered!" I shouted at Kowalski. "Now it's going to do that whole moon-bouncing thing and infect every dog in the world! Is this a double-cross? Or is it a triple-cross? I'm losing count."

Kowalski shook her head and shouted over the roar of the jetpacks.

"Nope. Kreem, or Agent 41 I should say, despite being a multimillionaire, could be a real cheapskate sometimes. To save money he used parts of an old vacuum cleaner to build the Secret Laser Machine. We just switched it from 'blow' to 'suck' and altered the direction slightly. Watch."

There was a change in the sound from the laser beam and it seemed to stop and then go into reverse. A bird caught in its path flew helplessly past us, sucked down towards the island, squawking and flapping.

I looked up ahead and saw two more specks getting dragged back. As the specks drew closer, I was pleased to see it was Agent 4 and Kliche struggling in the grip of the beam. Their jetpacks were useless against the pull of the Secret Laser Machine. I waved and grinned as they went past, and Agent 4 screamed, his face twisted in rage.

"You fools! My way was the only way! Help me! Heeeeeelllllpppppp!!!"

Kliche opened his mouth to shout something. I wanted to hear what it was, as it would have been the first time I had heard ol' Metal Mouth speak. But no sooner had he drawn breath than his set of steel gnashers were sucked out by the laser and spun helplessly down towards the island. Kliche's lips flapped around in the breeze and his shoulders slumped in defeat.

Agent 4's eyes popped as he caught sight of the cat formerly known as Kissy Karamba now dressed as Agent Kowalski.

"*You!*" he snarled. "I should have suspected something when you —"

We never found out exactly why he should have suspected Kowalski because at that moment he, too, was sucked out of range and back through the roof of his not-so-secret lair. There was a terrible grinding noise, then a sound like a herd of wild buffalo juggling an assortment of heavy car parts in a room full of jelly. Then there came a moment's silence before the secret lair erupted in a ball of flame and smoke and dust and rock.

We rocked in midair as the blast wave swept over us. I remembered something and turned to Kowalski in a panic.

"Hey! What about all those mutts in Kreem's lab?" I yelled. "They'll be fried!"

Kowalski shook her head.

"They were airlifted off the island about a half-hour back," she said. "Those 'dolphins' who gave you a ride? Special Cat Agents Dooble and Boffler, undercover dolphin patrol. They've been patrolling the island for weeks. They sprung the pooches when we knew that Agent 4 was going to launch the beam. We may be cats, but even we don't want to stand by and watch as dogs get fried."

Kowalski pointed to the horizon where a CIA RRU hovered next to another military-looking chopper.

"I took the liberty of calling in some backup. One's yours and one's a Cat's Whisker Search and Rescue vehicle."

She spoke into a concealed radio mike and the choppers buzzed across to pick us up. As we clambered aboard our separate aircraft I took one last look down at the smoking ruins, which were all that was left of Agent 4's mad plan.

I looked across at Kowalski and stuck up a paw.

"Thanks . . . cat," I yelled. "See you around."

"Not if I see you first, dog-breath," said Kowalski, smiling. And with that her chopper lifted into the air and she was gone. I sat back and the Reverend winked at me.

We had done it. We had saved the world. And we'd been saved by . . . a cat.

Great.

CHAPTER 12

TOMORROW NEVER DIES

After making the doggy world safe for all pooches, mutts, hounds, dawgs, and all things generally canine, I figured that the least the CIA could do was to make me, like, Dog President or something. The Reverend could be my faithful second in command, of course.

But do you know what we got out of all this from the CIA? Absolutely zip, my friends. Nothing. Nada. Not even so much as a box of Scooby Snax.

We were greeted by Mr. Don't himself when we got back to HQ, but he was only there to make sure we gave back all our CIA gadgets and gizmos before they booted us back into Z-Block. Mr. Smith explained it all to us in small words so that even I could follow it.

"The CIA must continue its top secret work," he said, facing us in a small room deep in the CIA bunker. "No two-legger must ever know about the work we do. They'd panic if they ever realized how clever we really are. Things must go on as normal. The CIA *is* grateful for all the help you've given us, even though we'll be working for some time to come to get Mr. Jimberlake back on MTV. He's not dealing with all this very well. And we have a whole bunch of dogs acting up. I guess until all the stocks of Kreemy Dog Food run out we'll just have to deal with that. But in the meantime, you guys are gong to have to go back to Z-Block, I'm afraid."

"Now wait just a minute, brother," said Bentley. "You ain't go —"

He didn't finish because Mr. Smith produced a small, penlike object from a pocket and put on a pair of sunglasses.

"Hey," I said. "I've seen this movie! You're going to —"

"Perform a complete memory wipe on you," he said, nodding. "Where do you think those MIB got the idea from? When I press this, it will clean all your memories of everything unusual you have seen or heard in the past few days."

He pressed the top of the pen and there was a blinding flash.

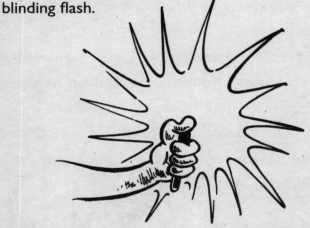

We woke up back in the yard at Z-Block. Well, I woke up; Bentley was still happily snoring in a heap next to me. I shook my head and tried to remember exactly what had happened.

It all came back instantly. Smith's memory-wipe hadn't worked on me because I'd closed my eyes when he'd pressed the pen thing. I'd watched the

Men In Black movies and always wondered why people didn't just close their eyes when they did that memory-wipe. And you know what? It worked.

It must still have knocked us cold, though, because here we were, back at the Pound.

Bentley grunted and came around slowly. He rubbed the back of his head. "Man, I feel like I've been knocked stupid," he said.

"CAN — YOU — RE-MEM-BER — ANY-THING?" I said in a voice you might use to an aged relative. Bentley slapped me across the chops.

"Of course I can remember," he said and pointed at his shades. "I'm wearing these, right? I seen *MIB*, too, you know."

Across the yard came a familiar figure carrying a tray. It was Fester. My heart sank. Fester liked nothing more than making our lives a misery and I was betting he was itching to pick up right where he'd left off. As he got closer I could see that he looked . . . different somehow, changed. His eyes were glazed and he had a weird smile on his spotty face.

"Hello my special little friends," he said in a far-away voice. "I see you are back from going through the green door and I suppose that I should be wondering how you got back because once you go through that door, dogs don't normally come back, do they? But, you know, I don't really care about all that because I want to make sure that you precious little furry fellers are having a nice time and I've brought you some lunch."

He drew a breath and set down the tray in front of us. On it were two gigantic rib-eye steaks with all the trimmings. Two bowls of ice-cold milk stood next to the plates.

"Please," said the new, all-weird Fester, "enjoy."

With that he slowly turned and walked away.

"I guess that mind-wipe thing worked pretty good on him," I said, tucking my starched white linen table napkin under my chin.

"I don't think it'll last, brother," said Bentley.

"Then let's enjoy it," I said, scooping up a mighty fistful of prime beef and cramming it into my open mouth. I sat back and smiled.

"What's so funny?" said Bentley, taking a swallow of milk.

I produced a diamond I'd saved from the deck of *Thunderpuss* and held it up to the sun.

"Oh, nothing," I said. "I was just thinking that I never did get around to handing this little baby in to the CIA."

"You know," said Bentley thoughtfully, "with a rock like that, two dogs could travel an awful long way from here."

"Amen to that Reverend," I said. "Which is why I grabbed a whole bunch of 'em while I had the chance."

I opened my other hand and dropped eight or nine of the finest diamonds in the world onto the dust, a big smile on my face.

"But where've you been keeping those?" asked Bentley.

I winced and shuffled my rear end painfully.

"Oh," said Bentley. "I see."

He paused for a minute then smiled.

"If this was a movie, you know what the Arnie line would be?" he said. "You know, the 'I'll be back' line."

I nodded and delivered the pay-off line.

"I guess you could say that I look like a cat that's got the Kreem."

We picked up our milk bowls and clinked them together.

"Ha ha ha ha ha ha!" cackled Bentley.

"Ha ha ha ha ha ha ha ha!" I cackled. I could get used to this evil genius stuff.